* * * * * * *

The old man walked ahead of the four of us. I found myself watching him. At first there didn't seem to be anything unusual about him, other than the fact that he seemed to be alone. I did notice that as he boarded the ship he glanced back toward us and then quickly turned back around.

The stranger was fairly tall and stood rather straight for a man as old as he appeared to be. He had a gray beard and mustache and a full head of hair that was gray like his beard. He was dressed nicely, but casual.

I couldn't decide if he turned away from us because he didn't want us to think he was being nosey, or if he was afraid that we might recognize him. I thought that I might be thinking in those terms as a result of having been a police officer for so many years. I made a mental note of him and filed it away in the back of my mind not knowing if I would ever need it.

As he disappeared around the corner of the passageways, I turned my attention back to the beautiful woman that was holding onto my arm. When I looked at Monica, she smiled up at me. I returned her smile. If she sensed that I had not been giving her my full attention, she didn't say anything.

* * * * * * *

Other titles by J.E. Terrall

Western Short Stories
  The Old West
  The Frontier
  Untamed Land
  Tales from the Territory

Western Novels
  Conflict in Elkhorn Valley
  Lazy A Ranch (A Modern
    Western)
  The Story of Joshua Higgins

Romance Novels
  Balboa Rendezvous
  Sing for Me
  Return to Me
  Forever Yours

Mystery/Suspense/Thriller
  I Can See Clearly
  The Return Home
  The Inheritance

Nick McCord Mysteries
  Vol – 1 Murder at Gill's Point
  Vol – 2 Death of a Flower
  Vol – 3 A Dead Man's Treasure
  Vol – 4 Blackjack, A Game to Die For
  Vol – 5 Death on the Lakes
  Vol – 6 Secrets Can Get You Killed

Peter Blackstone Mysteries
  Murder in the Foothills
  Murder on the Crystal Blue
  Murder of My Love

Frank Tidsdale Mysteries
  Death by Design
  Death by Assassination

DEATH ON THE LAKES

A Nick McCord Mystery
Vol 5

by
J. E. Terrall

ISBN: 978-0-9963951-0-6

This is a work of fiction. Names, characters, and incidents
are either a product of the author's imagination or are used
fictitiously, and any resemblance to actual persons, living or
dead, is purely coincidental.

Printed in the United States of America
First Printing / 2009 www.lulu.com
Second Printing / 2015 – wwwcreatspace.com

Cover: by J.E. Terrall

Book Layout/
Formatting: J.E. Terrall
               Custer, South Dakota

DEATH ON THE LAKES

A Nick McCord Mystery

To Eleanor Luze

CHAPTER ONE

The weather was looking pretty nice over Lake Mendota. The sun was shining and there was a gentle breeze coming in off the lake. There were several boats with bright white sails capturing the breeze as they sailed around the lake.

It was mid afternoon and Monica had gone off to get some groceries. I had been working in our home office. I had decided to take a break from setting up the new computer that Monica and I had purchased and were going to be using in our business as private investigators.

While relaxing during a short break on the balcony, I picked up the local Sunday newspaper from the table beside the lounge chair and began looking through it.

When I came to the travel section, I noticed an ad for an eight-day cruise around three of the Great Lakes. I found the picture of the boat in the ad to be fascinating. It reminded me of the cruise ships I had seen in television ads for cruises to Alaska or to the Bahamas, but maybe a bit smaller.

The thought occurred to me that a romantic cruise on the Great Lakes would be the perfect place to have our wedding and honeymoon all wrapped up in one package. After all, I had asked Monica to marry me and she had said "yes". We had some money coming in, and it would be the perfect way to use at least part of it. The timing could not have been better. We had nothing scheduled for sometime, and we were not ready to begin advertising for business.

It was at that moment that I heard Monica come in. I neatly folded the paper and set it on the table so that the ad would be where she could see it. I then got up and went into the kitchen.

"Hi. What have you been doing?" Monica asked as she started to empty the grocery bags.

"I've been thinking about you," I replied as I leaned over and kissed her lightly on the cheek.

"That's nice. Was there anything in particular that you were thinking?"

"As a matter of fact, yes," I said as I handed her a head of lettuce from the grocery bag.

"Ooooh, that sounds interesting. Am I going to like it?" she asked as she put the lettuce in the refrigerator.

"I sure hope so."

"Are you going to tell me what it is, or do I have to guess?"

"How about coming out on the balcony with me," I suggested.

I took her by the hand and led her out onto the balcony. I sat down and motioned for her to join me. She smiled as she sat down on my lap and slipped her hand around behind my neck.

"I have something to show you," I said, then reached for the paper.

I showed her the ad and gave her a minute or so to look at it. After a couple of minutes, she looked at me as if to ask what I had in mind.

"I was thinking that we could take a Great Lakes cruise and get married on board the ship. We could go as Nick McCord and Monica Barnhart, and return as Mr. and Mrs. McCord. It could be our wedding and honeymoon all rolled into one. What do you think?" I asked.

Monica looked at me, and then looked at the ad again. I couldn't tell what she was thinking. Slowly, a soft sexy smile came over her face.

"I think it would be terrific. It sounds so romantic," she said as she threw her arms around my neck and began kissing me.

After several minutes of some rather heavy necking, she leaned back and looked down at me. She was so excited that it was hard for her to contain herself.

"Wow. If I had known I was going to get that kind of a reaction, I would have suggested this a long time ago," I said.

"Better late then never," she said with a smile.

"I was thinking that we could ask Tom Walker to be my best man. What do you think?"

"I think that would be great."

"Who would you like to be your maid of honor?"

"I think I would like to ask Pamela Pierce."

"That's who I thought you would choose," I said with a grin. "Under the circumstances, I don't think we can really expect them to pay for their part of the cruise."

"I agree."

"I thought that we would pay for them. What do you think?"

"I think that's a great idea. It shouldn't be a problem. We have a pretty good check coming from Games Unlimited. We could use part of it for the cruise," Monica suggested.

"That's what I was thinking. Then it's settled?" I asked.

"Yes, yes," she said as she hugged and kissed me again and again.

We spent most of the evening talking about the cruise and going over the ad. We sort of set up an itinerary for the next couple of days.

* * * *

The next morning we began the task of working out the details of our cruise. I called my long time friend Tom at his Gill's Point Lodge near Gill's Rock, Wisconsin, to see if he could get away for a few days to take a cruise. Of course, I had to tell him why. I also told him that he would be keeping an eye on a very lovely and very single young woman that would be going along, and that she was

Monica's maid of honor. Tom thought it was nice of us to provide him with a date while on the cruise.

Monica called Pamela and quickly found that she wouldn't miss it for the world. She was told a little about the man she would be meeting on the cruise, especially the part about him being very handsome and single. Monica also told her that he owned a vacation lodge in upper Wisconsin. Since she was currently not involved with anyone, she thought that would be nice to have someone to tour the sights with at the different stops the ship would make.

After that was all settled, we contacted a travel agent and made the arrangements for the cruise. It would be four weeks before we would be leaving. That would give us time to get everything arranged so that we could get married aboard the ship. It would also give us the time we would need to get everything put together so that we could jump right into our investigation business as soon as we returned from the cruise.

The next four weeks went rather fast. Our check from Games Unlimited came through as expected and it was for more than we had expected. They had added a pretty hefty bonus since we had saved them a lot of money and prevented one of their games from being sold to a competitor. They also promised to contact us again if they ever found a need of our services. All was ready for our luxury cruise and our wedding.

* * * *

The four of us had agreed that we would meet at the dock in Chicago on the day of our departure. Monica and I arrived about two hours before sailing time and found Tom waiting for us. He was relaxing in the lounge.

Tom stood up as soon as he saw us. As he began walking toward us, I noticed that he had a big smile on his face. He looked like he was ready to enjoy himself.

"Hi, Tom." I said.

"Good to see you, again," he said as he stuck out his hand in greeting.

After we shook hands, he turned to Monica and gave her a big hug. From the look on her face, I don't think she had expected such a greeting.

"I see you finally got this big lug to marry you," Tom said as he let go of her and stepped back.

"Well, not yet, but the rope is getting a little tighter around his neck with each passing day," she said with a grin.

"Great. He needs someone like you to keep him in line. By the way, where's this lovely lady that I'm supposed to keep an eye on while you two are, shall we say, enjoying your first days of marital bliss?"

"I haven't seen her yet. She should be here soon." Monica said with a smile. "She said that she would be here on time, which is not one of her better traits, by the way."

"I see," Tom said with a slight grin.

"How have things been going at the lodge since we were up there?" I asked.

"They're going great. I've been busy ever since. I'm full all the time. I've even had to hire more help. I have a manager now. It frees me up so that I can do things like go on cruises to make sure my best friend gets married," he said with a grin.

"That's great. I'm glad to see that whole mess didn't hurt your business," I said.

"It didn't hurt it at all," he said, then turned to Monica.

"Say, Monica, what's this I hear about you going into business with Nick?"

"It's true. We are going to go full steam ahead as soon as we get back," Monica replied as she squeezed my arm and looked up at me.

"If you really want to know, she's already been working on a couple of cases with me," I said, my pride in her showing.

"Yeah. So I've heard," Tom replied. "That's great."

"Nick, when do we board?" Monica asked.

"I think we can board almost any time. Do you want to wait for Pamela here?"

"I've got the feeling we won't have to wait long," Tom said as he looked over Monica's shoulder. "Is that Pamela?"

Monica and I turned to look. Coming across the lounge was a tall, slim woman with long dark brown hair and a beautiful smile. The summer dress she was wearing revealed the fact that she had a very nice figure. Her skirt swayed with every step she took on her long shapely legs.

I glanced over at Tom. It was clear that he found her to be very attractive. I was glad to see he hadn't lost his ability to recognize a beautiful woman when he saw one. I nudged Monica. She turned and looked at Tom. She smiled as if to say, "I knew they would hit it off".

"That's her," Monica said with a smile.

"She's beautiful," Tom said in almost a whisper.

Tom was immediately taken with Pamela. I could not remember when he had been so dumbstruck by a pretty woman. There was no doubt in my mind that it was going to be an interesting trip. Little did I know just how interesting it would be.

"Pamela, this is Tom Walker. Tom, this is Pamela Pierce," Monica said.

"Hello," Pamela said as she smiled at Tom.

"Hello," Tom replied, never taking his eyes off hers.

They stood there and looked at each other. It looked as if Tom might have met the first woman that could steal his heart.

"Excuse me," Monica said to them.

Tom and Pamela suddenly looked at Monica as if they were surprised that she was even there.

"Pamela, this is Nick," she said.

"Oh. Hi, Nick," she replied, looking a bit embarrassed.

"Hi, Pamela," I replied with a smile.

"Is your luggage checked in?" Monica asked.

"Yes. It should have been taken to my cabin," Tom replied.

"Mine, too," Pamela said, looking back at Tom.

"Monica and I have a suite on Deck four. The suite number is four-twenty-two," I said. "Your cabins should be near our suite."

"I have cabin number four-twenty," Pamela said.

"I have cabin number four-twenty-one, right next door," Tom said with a smile.

"That's not right," Monica said, her face suddenly turning serious. "Cabin four-twenty-one is on the opposite side of the ship from our suite."

"Are you sure," Tom asked.

"Yes. I remember looking at the deck plans and noticed all even numbered cabins are on one side and all the odd numbered cabins are on the other."

"She's right. I'll see what I can do to get the two of you in cabins next to each other, that is if you would prefer that?" I asked with a smile.

Tom looked at Pamela, and she looked at him. They looked as if they were hoping that the other one would speak up first. It was clear that neither of them wanted it to be too obvious, but it was easy to tell that they wanted their cabins to be close.

"I think that would be nice. It would be better if we were all in the same area, don't you think?" Tom asked as he looked at Pamela while trying very hard to make it sound so logical.

"Yes, I agree," Pamela added. "It would be better if we were all together."

"If you will excuse me, I'll go see what can be done about getting Tom moved to the same side of the ship," I said.

"If you ladies don't mind waiting here, I'll go along with Nick," Tom said.

"Sure," Pamela said with a smile.

In a matter of a few steps, Tom had caught up with me. We walked side by side toward the ticket counter.

After explaining the problem to the woman at the ticket counter, it didn't take her but a couple of minutes to make the necessary changes. It seemed that the gentleman who they had assigned to cabin four-eighteen had not arrived yet. Since he had not reserved a specific cabin, it would only take a few minutes to move Tom's luggage to the other cabin, and place the gentleman's luggage in cabin four-twenty-one.

After thanking the ticket clerk, we started walking back across the lounge to rejoin the women. I noticed Tom was looking at an older man. From the expression on Tom's face, I got the impression that he might know the old man. Tom looked like he wanted to say something. Instead he turned and looked toward the women without commenting.

"Did you get the cabin changed?" Pamela asked, directing her question to Tom.

"Yes, we did. I will be right next door to you in cabin four-eighteen," Tom replied."

"I think that will be nice," Pamela said with a smile.

"I think we should get aboard," I said. "Tom might need to help move some of his luggage to his new cabin,"

"Good idea," Tom agreed.

Pamela smiled up at Tom as he took hold of her hand. They started across the lounge to the ship's docking gate. I took Monica by the hand and we followed Tom and Pamela.

Just as we were approaching the gate to the dock, that same old man passed in front of Tom. I noticed that Tom sort of hesitated for just a split second as if something was bothering him. Tom watched the man turn and go through the gate. I didn't get to see the man's face, but once again I got the feeling that Tom thought he might know him, but that he wasn't sure.

The man walked ahead of the four of us. I found myself watching him. At first there didn't seem to be anything unusual about him, other than the fact that he seemed to be alone. I did notice that as he boarded the ship he glanced back toward us and then quickly turned back around.

The stranger was fairly tall and stood rather straight for a man as old as he appeared to be. He had a gray beard and mustache and a full head of hair that was gray like his beard. He was dressed nicely, but casually.

I couldn't decide if he turned away from us because he didn't want us to think he was being nosey, or if he was afraid that we might recognize him. I thought that I might be thinking in those terms as a result of having been a police officer for so many years. I made a mental note of him and filed it away in the back of my mind not knowing if I would ever need it.

As he disappeared around the corner of the passageways, I turned my attention back to the beautiful woman that was holding onto my arm. When I looked at Monica, she smiled up at me. I returned her smile. If she sensed that I had not been giving her my full attention, she didn't say anything.

* * * *

When we got to our suite, we left Pamela and Tom to go to their cabins and get settled in. I opened the door to our suite and stepped back so Monica could go in first.

"Wow," she said as her breath caught. "This is lovely."

I watched her as she slowly moved into the suite and looked around. The suite was larger than the cabins and had a sitting area away from the bed. After a couple of minutes of looking around, she came up to me and threw her arms around my neck.

"This is wonderful," she said as she kissed me.

CHAPTER TWO

After a long and wonderful kiss, Monica and I took a few minutes to get our bags unpacked. It didn't take us long to get settled in a little.

As soon as we had done as much as we were going to do for the moment, I took Monica by the hand and led her over to the bed. We laid down on the large king-size bed. Monica rolled up against me and rested her head on my shoulder. She didn't say anything right away. I had no idea what she was thinking, but I was thinking about the woman lying beside me. I could hardly believe that we were finally going to get married.

"Nick?"

"Yeah, Honey?"

"I've never been as happy as I am right now," she whispered.

"I'm glad. I certainly don't know what you see in me, but whatever it is, I'm glad you do."

I turned my head toward her. She rose up off my shoulder and kissed me. It was not a passionate kiss, the kind that was meant to stir up the deepest of desires, but rather one that was meant to show her deep love for me.

It should have been a time of quiet tenderness that would allow us to relax and be comfortable in each other's arms and with each other, but the knocking on our door took that away. I looked into Monica's eyes.

"If I have to guess who is knocking at our door, my guess would be it is Pamela and Tom," I said.

"I'm sure you're right. Are you going to answer the door?"

"Do I have to?"

"I think you should."

"Okay," I replied.

I was reluctant to leave my comfortable place on the bed with Monica. She rolled away from me and sat up on the edge of the bed as I rolled over to the other side. I got up and went to the door. I looked back over my shoulder to make sure that Monica was presentable before I opened it. She nodded that she was ready.

I reached out and pulled the door open. Tom and Pamela were standing in the passageway. They were both grinning from ear to ear as if they knew something that we didn't. I turned and looked at Monica as if to say, "I told you so". She grinned in reply.

"We hope we are not disturbing you two, but we thought you might like to go up on deck and watch the ship sail out of port," Tom said.

"Sounds like a good idea to me," Monica said as she came up behind me and slipped her arm around my waist.

"I guess that settles that," I said with a smile.

I stepped back out of the way and let Monica go out the door. After locking our suite behind me, we followed Tom and Pamela down the passageway to a carpeted stairway that went up to the Sun Deck.

I noticed Tom had hold of Pamela's hand as they walked in front of us. I had to wonder why they wanted us to go with them. They seemed to be so engrossed in each other that I doubted they had any idea that we were only a few steps behind them.

Once on the Sun Deck, Monica and I walked over to the railing and looked down at the dock below. There were still several people coming aboard the ship. We could also see that luggage was still being loaded aboard the ship.

While looking over the side of the ship, I noticed the old man that had boarded the ship ahead of us. He was walking slowly down the gangplank as if he was leaving the ship. Since he had just boarded the ship, I had to wonder why he was getting off. My first thought was that he had forgotten something.

While leaning against the railing, I watched him as he walked over to the officer who was checking passengers aboard. The old man looked worried about something, but from where I was standing it was really hard to tell.

I couldn't hear the discussion, but I got the impression that things were not going the way the old man would have liked. All I could think of was that he might not have liked his accommodations. That didn't seem likely to me, as the cabins were as nice as any hotel I've ever stayed in.

It also occurred to me that he might have changed his mind about going on the cruise. However, there was little chance that he had not planned his trip for some time. These cruises were not the kind that one schedules at the last minute. Reservations usually had to be made weeks in advance, although I was sure that there were always exceptions.

I watched him as he looked toward the ship, then back toward the ticket office. He did that several times before he finally turned and looked at the ship one last time. It looked as if he couldn't make up his mind if he should go back aboard the ship or not.

He must have decided to board the ship because he started back up the gangplank. However, his movements indicated that he was reluctant to return to the ship. He moved rather slowly as if he was not sure he had made the right decision.

Monica disturbed my thoughts when she reached over and put her arm around my waist. I turned and looked at her.

"It's a beautiful day to go out on the lake, don't you think?" Monica asked as she squeezed me around the waist.

"Yes." I replied, still not giving her my full attention.

"What's the matter? Are you having second thoughts?" Monica asked.

I could hear the concern in her voice and could see it in her eyes. I wasn't sure if I should say anything about the old man or not. I didn't want to ruin even a minute of the trip for her. Besides, what was I going to tell her? I didn't know who the old man was or anything else about him. Whatever his problem was, it was his business and didn't happen to be any of mine.

"No. No second thoughts, Honey. I guess I was just thinking about where we are going," I replied as I smiled at her.

"And where are we going?" she asked.

"We are starting out on the greatest journey of our lives," I replied as I leaned down and kissed her lightly on the lips.

I gently squeezed her hand and looked into her eyes as she smiled up at me. She seemed to accept my reply without hesitation. We both turned back and looked out over the city of Chicago. It was a beautiful day. It was a day that should not be wasted on anything other than ourselves. The sky was clear and blue. A breeze last night had cleared away the gray haze that often hangs over the city.

"Hey, you two," I heard Tom call out.

As we turned and looked at him, he took our picture. We smiled and he took another.

"Give me that camera," I said. "I'll take a picture of you and Pamela."

Tom stepped toward me and handed me his camera. I waited until he moved back next to the rail with Pamela at his side. I noticed that Tom put his arm around Pamela's narrow waist and drew her close to him. From the look on Pamela's face, I was sure that she didn't mind the attention she was getting from him. In fact, she looked as if she enjoyed being close to him.

After I took a couple of pictures of them, I gave the camera back to Tom and turned toward Monica. She was standing at the rail looking out over the city. I moved up behind her and wrapped my arms around her. She put her hands over mine and leaned back against me.

"We should be shoving off in a little bit," I whispered in her ear.

"I know."

Monica and I stood by the railing of the Sun Deck and watched as the crew of the ship prepared to depart from the dock. As the lines were cast off and the ship began to move away from the dock, I could not help but think of how pleasant this trip could be. When we return to this port, we would return as Mr. and Mrs. Nicholas McCord, I thought. The idea that we would be husband and wife caused me to gently squeeze her.

The weather was almost perfect. There was a slight breeze, but it was almost nullified by the movement of the ship as it pulled away from the dock. The sky was clear except for a couple of fluffy white clouds that slowly drifted across the royal blue sky. Lake Michigan had never looked so clear and clean as it did at that moment. There was hardly a ripple in the water as the ship moved smoothly across it.

The morning was warm and the sun was bright. It was a perfect day to spend some time on the Sun Deck soaking up some sun. I, for one, had never been much for lying around in the sun. Monica with her fair skin could burn fairly easily. But I had to admit that it was still a nice day to enjoy the outdoors.

"Say, you two," Tom called out. "Pamela and I are going to get into our swimsuits and take a dip in the pool. You care to join us?"

I looked at Monica. She sort of shrugged her shoulders as if to say that she wouldn't mind, but it was all right with her if we didn't go for a swim.

"Okay, for a little while," I replied.

Tom and Pamela turned and headed toward the stairway that would take them down to the fourth deck where their cabins were located. We followed along behind. I could not help but notice that Tom and Pamela seemed to be getting along very well. Tom had his arm around her narrow waist and she had her arm around him as they walked along the passageways.

"Looks to me like Tom and Pamela are hitting it off pretty well," Monica said with a smile.

"Yeah, it does. But I think it's too early to tell."

"Where's your sense of romance?" Monica asked looking up at me.

"I'm saving it all for you," I replied as I gave her a slight squeeze.

* * * *

As we walked down the passageway toward our suite, we could see Tom and Pamela stop at Pamela's cabin door. Tom stood with her in front of her door for a minute or so. We could not hear what he was saying to her, but it was clear that she was listening intently to him. Tom had her hand in his. He leaned close to her and kissed her lightly on the lips. From where we were, it looked like things were moving pretty fast between them. Maybe a little too fast, I thought.

"It appears you are right. They have hit it off pretty well," I said to Monica as I turned and slipped the key into the door of our suite.

I opened the door and waited for Monica to go in first. She had a worried look on her face as she moved past me into the suite. I glanced down the passageway in time to see Tom go into his cabin before I stepped inside our suite.

"What's the matter?" I asked Monica as I moved across the room toward her.

"I hope Pamela isn't falling too hard for Tom," she said softly.

"Why? That's what I thought you wanted for her."

"I do, but - - - ."

"But what?"

"Pamela got hurt once before, I don't want her to get hurt again."

"Come on. She's a big girl. No one gets through life without getting a few bruises along the way. I think she can take care of herself," I said trying to be a little reassuring.

"But you don't know her like I do," Monica protested.

"That's very true. But don't you think that it would be better for you to be there for her if things don't work out, than to get in the way of her possibly finding some happiness with Tom?" I asked.

"You're telling me to mind my own business, aren't you?" she asked with a surprised look on her face.

I thought for a moment, as I looked at her.

"Yes, I guess I am. It's all right to worry a little about her, but don't get in the way."

She walked over to me, closing the distance between us. As she got close to me, she reached up and put her hands on my shoulders. I reached out and put my hands on her hips and gently drew her to me.

"You are my business, aren't you?" she whispered as she looked up at me.

"I sure hope so," I said as I looked into her deep blue eyes.

"What do you say to giving Tom a call and telling him we will see them at lunch," Monica said in her sexy voice as she looked into my eyes and pressed her body against me.

"I think that is a wonderful idea," I replied as I gently squeezed her.

"But you have to kiss me first," she said.

I didn't bother to think about that. I simply drew her body tightly up against me. She slid her hands around to the back of my head as she tipped her head to one side. Our lips met in a long hard passionate kiss that was meant to say, "I need you". The feel of the passion in her kiss and the feel of her firm body pressing against me was enough to convince me that she really wanted to be with me, alone.

When we finally broke off the kiss, we were both breathing heavily. A smile came over her face as we looked into each other's eyes.

"Wow," she said in a husky whisper.

"Yeah. I better make that call before they come knocking on our door," I said, still holding her tightly.

"Good idea."

I reluctantly let go of Monica and stepped back to look at her. It took me a minute to think about what I was going to say to Tom, but looking at Monica I realized that Tom would understand. If he didn't, he wasn't the man I thought him to be. Besides, if I knew him, he would be too busy with Pamela to even miss us.

I went over to the chair next to the phone and sat down. I placed a call to Tom's cabin. It was answered quickly.

"Hello?"

"Tom, this is Nick."

"Yeah. What's up?"

"Monica and I won't be joining you and Pamela at the pool."

"Oh. Is something wrong?"

"No. Everything is very right. You two enjoy yourselves, and we'll meet you for lunch in the restaurant."

"Okay, but we will miss you," Tom said.

"I seriously doubt that. The two of you look like you're getting along just fine."

"We are. She's a wonderful woman."

"I'm sure she is. Have a good time, Tom. We'll see you at lunch."

"Okay."

As I hung up the phone, I looked over at Monica. She looked as if she were waiting for me to tell her what Tom said.

"Tom said that they would miss us," I said with a smile.

"I doubt that," Monica replied with a grin.

"That's what I told him. Now what about us?"

"I think it's time for us to start making the most of this beautiful suite, especially this great big bed," she said as she reached out and lightly touched the bed.

"I couldn't agree with you more," I said as I stepped up in front of her and took her in my arms.

She wrapped her arms around me, leaned up against me and smiled. I knew that this morning was going to be one that I was not likely to forget.

It didn't take us long to get each other undressed and to fall into each other's arms on the bed. The feel of her soft smooth skin under my hands, and the feel of her body pressing against me were more than I could handle. We quickly shut out the rest of the world. We let our love and desire for each other take over.

CHAPTER THREE

Monica and I had spent the morning in our suite. Although I had lived with her for some time now, I had never shared a more precious or intimate time with her. It would have been nice if we could have stayed in the suite for the entire day, but I was getting hungry.

It was getting on toward time to meet Tom and Pamela for lunch. We took a shower together that lasted much longer then we had planned. It took us a while to get dressed, but that was probably because we didn't really want to let go of our time together. We dressed casually for lunch, then left our suite for the restaurant on deck three, one deck below the one our suite was on.

When we arrived at the restaurant, we stopped in the entryway and looked out over the dining room. Although I was looking for Tom and Pamela, I couldn't help noticing the beauty of the room. The tables were lined up in neat rows with linen table clothes and napkins that stood tall like miniature white pyramids on white sand. The silverware sparkled as did the long stem crystal wine goblets and water glasses. The walls and the ceiling were of polished walnut. It gave the room a special elegance that was typical of only the finest of ships or hotels.

"Do you see them?" Monica asked disturbing my thoughts.

"Ah, yes. They are over there," I said as I pointed toward a table across the room next to a window.

"I see them," she replied and began walking in their direction. I followed along behind her.

"Hi," Pamela said with a big grin. "We weren't sure if you were going to come up for air."

"Isn't this beautiful," Monica said as she looked around while I pulled a chair back for her.

It was clear that Monica was going to ignore Pamela's remark. I sure wasn't going to comment on it.

"It is," Pamela replied.

"I think I can get some ideas for my lodge from this ship," Tom said as he looked around the room.

"Possible," I replied. "I don't know about the rest of you, but I would like to eat."

"I can see where staying in your suite all morning could make a guy real hungry," Tom said with a slight chuckle.

"It can make a girl hungry, too," Monica added with a knowing smile.

The waiter's timing couldn't have been better. He suddenly appeared and was ready to take our order for lunch. It seemed like only a few seconds after he left with our order when another waiter showed up with our coffee.

We all settled into casual conversation while we waited for our meals. I could hear the girls enough to know that they were talking about the upcoming wedding. Meanwhile, Tom and I talked about his lodge and how things had been going.

When our meals arrived, we all slowed down on the conversation and spent a good deal of time eating. We were all pretty hungry and the food was excellent. I had no idea what Tom and Pamela had done all morning, but there was no lack of appetite on their part, either.

As I finished eating my last bite of food, I looked up and saw Tom looking off across the room. It seemed that he was engrossed in whatever it was he was looking at. From the look on his face, I got the feeling that he was trying to recall something. It was almost as if he had seen someone from his past that reminded him of an unpleasant experience.

I turned and looked in the direction that Tom was staring. Once again I saw that same old man that I had seen on the dock earlier. He was just entering the dining room.

When I turned and looked at him, I noticed that he quickly turned away. That was the second time he had turned away when I looked at him. It was as if he were trying to hide his face from me.

I watched as the man was led to a table in a corner on the other side of the room. There was something about him that made it hard for me not to stare at him.

When the hostess pulled back a chair for him, he pulled out a different chair and sat down on it. I found it interesting that he had chosen to sit with his back to the room even though the hostess had selected a chair that would have allowed him to look out over the room.

Sitting the way he had chosen put his back toward us. That seemed kind of strange as it put him facing the wall. There was not much to see on that section of the wall as far as I could tell.

I turned back and looked at Tom again. He was still looking at the old man as if he should know who he was.

"Tom," I said, but he didn't immediately respond.

"Tom."

Tom turned and looked at me. He looked as if he had suddenly realized that he had been staring at the old man.

"Yeah," he replied as he realized that I was talking to him.

"What's the matter," I asked quietly so I wouldn't disturb the women.

"Nothing," he replied, but I got the feeling that there was something wrong.

"Do you know that old man?"

"I keep thinking that I do, but I can't seem to place him."

"Maybe he was a guest at your lodge at one time."

Tom glanced over at the man again, then said, "I suppose that's possible, but I usually remember my guests."

"Maybe he reminds you of someone you have met somewhere?"

"That could be. I'm sure I would have remembered that beard, though."

"What are you two talking about?" Monica asked.

"We're talking about the old man sitting over there in the corner, the one with his back to us," I said being as discreet as possible in pointing him out for them.

Monica and Pamela looked over toward the man. Monica didn't seem to notice anything unusual about him. With his back to us, I doubted that she would have recognized him even if she knew him, I certainly couldn't. Pamela looked like she might recognize him, but like Tom was not sure.

"Tom, isn't that the old man we saw in the passageway when we were going to our cabins after our swim?" Pamela asked in a whisper as she leaned closer to Tom.

"Yeah. I think so."

"What about him?" I asked.

"Tom and I were walking down the passageway toward our cabins. That old man was coming toward us. When we passed in the passageway I said "hi" to him, but he didn't say a word. He glanced at Tom then glanced at me, but kept on going.

"When we got to my cabin, Tom kissed me outside my door. As I turned to go into my cabin, I saw the old man standing near the stairway watching us. As soon as he realized that I was looking at him, he quickly ducked around the corner and went on up the stairs. I can tell you that it gave me goose bumps," she said with a slight shiver.

"I can certainly understand why he would look at you. You're a very pretty woman," Monica suggested as a way of explaining why he would be looking at her.

"No, I don't think that is why he was watching me. I'm not even sure that he was looking at me. He could have been looking at Tom. From that distance it was hard to tell."

I sat back in my chair to think about what had been said. I noticed Monica looking at me. From the expression on her face she seemed to be looking to me for answers. Answers to what, I had no idea.

I tried to put together everything that had been said and everything I had observed with regard to the old man, but I couldn't come up with anything that was cause for any of us to be concerned about him. There was no doubt that the old man had acted a little strange, but that was about it. He had done nothing to make me think that he might be a danger to any of us.

"I don't think there is anything to worry about from him, Tom. You will probably remember where you saw him before, or who he reminds you of when you least expect it," I said.

"I'm sure you're right, but why did he stop and look at us that way in the passageway?" Pamela asked.

"In what way?" I asked.

"I don't know, but it was strange."

"How was it strange?" I asked.

"I don't know, but I felt like he was looking right through me. It was almost as if he had wished that he had never seen me," Pamela said, then turned and looked at Tom as if she was looking to him to help her find the words she needed to explain how it made her feel.

"I wouldn't worry about it. It's probably nothing," Monica said, then glanced at me.

"I'm sure that he probably thinks that he knows Tom from somewhere and can't place him, either," I said.

"That's probably it," Tom agreed.

"Why don't you ask him now? It won't take but a minute, and it will ease your mind and mine," Pamela suggested.

"That's a good idea," Tom replied as he pushed back his chair and started across the room toward the man.

I wasn't as confident as Tom that Pamela's idea was a good one. On the other hand, the fact that we were in a large room with a good number of people around made it as good a time as any to clear up the matter.

Tom walked across the room toward the old man. As he approached him, Tom stepped to one side and looked down at him.

From where I was sitting, I could not hear what was being said, but it appeared as if it was a relatively normal conversation. I was not in a position to see the old man's reaction to Tom's interruption of his dinner. It took only a few minutes before Tom returned to the table.

"Well?" Pamela asked, impatient for Tom to tell her what he had said.

"Not much to say. His name is Oliver Higgins and he is from the New England area. He was not sure that he wanted to take this cruise, but his children had paid for it and he could hardly turn them down. He said that he didn't know who I was, but he thought that he might have seen me somewhere before."

"So he thought he knew you, too," Pamela said with a grin.

"Yeah. When I asked him if he had ever been in Wisconsin, he said that he had never been there."

Although Tom said nothing that would lead me to believe that Mr. Higgins might know Tom, I got the feeling that Tom still thought that he should know him. It also struck me as strange that a man from New England would be on a cruise that only covers three of the Great Lakes, and the most western ones at that.

As I listened to Tom, I looked over at Mr. Higgins. I noticed that he had hardly finished his dinner before he got up and left. Even though there was no reason to, I couldn't help but think about him. I had a gut feeling that he was not who he seemed to be, but then I didn't know who he was in the first place.

"Apparently we both thought that we looked like someone we knew," Tom said with a slight chuckle.

Even though I felt that there was more to it than I could see, I had to shake myself and remind myself that I was not on this ship as a detective or even as an investigator. There was no reason for me to think about anyone other than Monica. I didn't want anything to distract us on this cruise. This cruise was to be a very special time for us.

I turned and looked at Monica. I found her looking back at me. She had this look on her face that told me that she wanted to know what was on my mind. I smiled at her and hoped that she would pick up on my signals that I would talk to her about it later. Being the smart woman that she was, she smiled and winked as a way of saying, I love you and we'll talk later.

"Say, what do you say to going to the lounge and having a drink," Pamela suggested.

"Sounds all right to me," Tom agreed.

Monica looked over at me. I shrugged my shoulders to indicate that it was all right with me, too. We got up and left the restaurant.

We went to the lounge and spent the afternoon talking and playing Bridge. The time went by rather fast as we were all having a good time. It seemed like we had no more than started playing cards and it was almost time for dinner.

* * * *

As we were about ready to call it a day and return to our rooms to freshen up before dinner, a steward came over to our table.

"Mr. Walker?" he asked looking at me.

"I'm Tom Walker," Tom said before I had a chance to say anything.

"Mr. Walker, the man in the cabin where your personal belongs had been originally sent asked if you would mind going by to pick up one that was apparently left behind. It seems that a piece of luggage that belongs to you was left in the room. I would be most happy to get it for you, if you prefer."

"No, that's all right. We're on our way to our rooms now anyway. I can stop by and get it," Tom said.

"Thank you, sir," the steward said, then turned and left.

"I guess I'd better go see what it was that was left behind."

"You go on ahead, we'll escort Pamela to her cabin," I told him.

"Okay. I'll see you in a few minutes?" he asked Pamela.

"Give me a little time. I want to change into something special for you," she said with a smile.

Tom leaned down and kissed Pamela lightly on the lips, then left the lounge. I stood and pulled back the chair for Monica while Pamela stood up. We left the lounge and walked down the passageway to our suite. I stood at the door to our suite until Pamela had opened her door and was safely in her cabin, then I went inside.

Monica changed into a very nice, and I might add, very sexy evening dress for dinner. I put on a dark suit that was appropriate for an evening of dining and dancing on a luxury cruise ship.

* * * *

We joined Tom and Pamela in the restaurant for dinner. Again, it was an excellent meal. We then left the restaurant and went to the lounge for an evening of dancing. After a few dances and a few drinks, Monica and Pamela went off to the Ladies Room to "freshen up".

"Did you get what they left in the cabin?" I asked.

"Yeah. It was my briefcase."

"Why didn't the steward pick it up and take it to your cabin?"

"I'm not sure. I think the gentleman in the room didn't trust them with it. When they moved my luggage I guess they forgot my briefcase. To be honest I didn't even miss it."

"The way you've been spending time with Pamela, I'm not surprised," I said with a grin. "I'm surprised that you remember your name.

"Yeah. I guess I have been a little distracted by her. She is one hell of nice looking woman."

"I'll give her that. She seems nice, too. It looks to me as if the two of you are getting along okay."

"We are. I could get used to being around her," Tom said with a grin.

"Monica won't tell you this, but Pamela had a difficult relationship not too long ago. I would take it as a personal favor if you'd go easy."

"No problem, Nick. Whatever comes of this trip with her will be mutual. The last thing I want to do is hurt her. I already like her too much to want to hurt her in any way."

"Thanks. I know that Monica will be glad to hear that."

After the girls returned to the table, we spent the rest of the evening dancing and enjoying each other's company. When it was getting late, we decided to call it a night. The next day we would be on Mackinac Island. It would be a busy day with all there is to see on the island. I was looking forward to spending a quiet day of sightseeing and touring with Monica.

We decided that it was time to bid Tom and Pamela goodnight and left them in the passageway to say their goodnights. It didn't take us long to get into bed. Between the fresh air, a few drinks and some dancing I fell asleep with Monica curled up beside me shortly after my head fit the pillow.

CHAPTER FOUR

Deep in the recesses of my mind I thought I could hear the sound of a voice calling to me. The voice was almost inaudible as if it was someone very far away. I also thought I could feel someone touching me, but I was still not sure. Opening my eyes, I realized that it was Monica touching me on the shoulder.

"Nick. Nick."

"Yeah, Honey. Something wrong?"

"There's someone at the door."

It was then that I heard the knocking on the door again. I sat up in bed and looked at Monica. I glanced over at the clock on the bedside table. It was two-thirty in the morning. I couldn't imagine who would be knocking on our door at this ungodly hour. We hadn't been in bed for very long.

"Just a minute," I called out as I swung my legs over the side of the bed.

I grabbed a robe off the chair next to the bed and put it on as I walked through the sitting area to the door. I glanced back to make sure that Monica was covered before I unlocked the door and opened it. Standing in front of the door were two men in uniforms. One of them was a ship's steward and the other was a ship's officer.

"Yes, what is it?" I asked, my brain still not functioning clearly.

"Excuse me for bothering you, sir, but are you Mr. Nicholas McCord?" the officer asked politely.

"Yes. What do you want?" I asked wanting them to get to the point of why they had disturbed my rest.

"The Captain would like you to come with us, if you don't mind."

"But I do mind. Do you know what time it is?"

"Yes, sir. I'm afraid I do and I'm sorry for the lateness of the hour, but it's really very important. The Captain insists," the young officer said.

"I'm not going anywhere until you tell me what this is all about."

The officer looked at me for a moment. He then looked up and down the passageway as if to make sure that there was no one around who might be able to overhear him before he replied.

"Mr. McCord, there has been a murder on board the ship."

There was no question that woke my brain up. I was suddenly very alert and listening to what the officer had to say.

"The Captain said that he knows that you are a detective on the Milwaukee Police Department. He is requesting your help, sir."

"Well, I'm no longer a police officer. I'm a private investigator now."

"I'm sure that the Captain would still like to talk to you. He would appreciate any help that you could offer him in this matter," the officer said, the look on face seemed to be almost pleading for me to honor the Captain's request.

"Where did the murder take place?"

"In cabin two-sixty-one, sir."

"Two-sixty-one? Where is cabin two-sixty-one?"

"It is located two levels down from here on the starboard side of the ship forward of mid-ship, sir."

"Have the Captain seal off that cabin to everyone. I don't want anyone, and I mean anyone, in that cabin until I've had a chance to look around. Do you understand?"

"Yes, sir."

"Tell your Captain that I will be there as soon as I can get dressed."

"Yes, sir," he replied, then quickly turned around and left with the steward.

I watched him as he hurried away. As he disappeared around the corner, I closed the door and turned around. I could see Monica sitting up in the bed holding the sheet over her breasts. She looked very sexy, but it was the look on her face that caught and held my attention. I could see the concern in her eyes.

"What's going on?"

"The Captain has requested my help. It seems that there's been a murder on board the ship."

"A murder?"

"Yes."

"Who was killed?"

"I don't know, but I'm sure that I will find out very soon. I told the officer that I would come and take a look at the crime scene as soon as I could get dressed."

"What do you want me to do?"

"I want you to stay here and wait until I get back. I don't want you to leave the suite. I'll fill you in on everything as soon as I can."

"You promise?"

"Yes, of course. We're partners, aren't we?" I asked as I sat down on the edge of the bed.

She reached out and touched my arm as I leaned close to her. Our lips met and we shared a loving tender kiss.

As I drew back and looked into her eyes, I could see that she was concerned. I didn't see any reason for her to be, but it sort of made me feel loved.

"You better get going. The Captain is waiting," she whispered.

I stood up and got dressed. As soon as I was ready, I walked by the bed, leaned over and gave her a gentle kiss on the forehead.

"I'm not sure how long this will take."

"That's all right. Just be careful."

"I will," I replied, then turned and left our suite.

* * * *

The passageways were dimly lit, but there was enough light to make it easy to navigate them. I took the passageway to about mid-ship and descended down the stairway to Deck Two. I took the passageway that would take me to the starboard side of the ship then turned toward the bow.

As I turned the corner, I noticed several people standing in front of one of the cabins. There appeared to be three ship's officers and two ship's stewards. One of the men was the Captain of the ship. As soon as he saw me coming toward them, he stepped forward to introduce himself.

"Mr. McCord?" he asked.

"Yes."

"I'm Captain Klausen. I'm very pleased that you were willing to come at my request."

"No problem. What happened here?"

"It seems that a Mr. Frank Wright from Chicago was murdered in his cabin. The motive appears to be robbery."

"Who discovered the body?"

"One of our stewards. The one sitting on the chair over there," he said as he pointed to a man sitting next to the wall.

The man looked as if he was rather shaken. He had an officer standing next to him. The officer looked like he might be the ship's doctor.

"Has anyone been in the cabin?" I asked.

"Just the steward and the First Officer when he was called down here by the steward."

"Did they touch anything?

"I don't know. I doubt that they would."

"Has the doctor been in to check the body?"

"Oh, yes. He has been in the cabin, too. But all he did was confirm that the man was dead. I had already instructed him not to touch anything in the room."

"Good. I think it would be a good idea if you took the steward and First Officer somewhere quiet and got statements from them. The sooner the better. The longer we wait to get a statement, the less likely we are to get good accurate information on what they saw in the cabin, as well as what they saw outside the cabin. Remember, every detail is important no matter how unimportant it may seem."

"I'll take care of that. Anything else?"

"I'll want to talk to them after I've had a chance to look over the cabin."

"Of course," the Captain replied.

"I would also like to have the ship's doctor stay here with me. I may need his help in determining the cause of death."

"Certainly."

"It would be best if we can clear the passageway of all unnecessary personnel. The more people we have standing around the more likely this is going to attract attention. I would prefer that knowledge of what happened here be kept to a minimum for now," I said to the Captain.

"Yes, that would be best. I'll take everyone to the Officers' Mess and get started on taking their statements. I'll leave Doctor Stillman here with you. He can show you the way to the Officers' Mess when you're finished."

"By the way, be sure to record their statements," I said, then I turned and looked toward the cabin.

"Yes, of course," the Captain said, but I was already preparing myself for what I might see in the cabin.

As I stepped up to the door of cabin two-sixty-one, I could hear Captain Klausen giving orders to those in the passageway. The cabin door was almost closed. I pushed open the door and looked inside the cabin. My first thought was that a tornado had gone through the place. The entire cabin was a mess. This brought to mind a couple of things.

The first one was that there had been a struggle in the cabin. Since the cabin seemed to be more of a mess than one would expect to see in a struggle, I determined that the cabin had most likely been ransacked as well. There were only two reasons to ransack a room. One was the person who committed the crime was looking for something and had no idea where it had been hidden. The other reason was to hide evidence, or at least make evidence more difficult to find, therefore making it harder to establish who had committed the crime.

The body of the victim was lying on the floor beside the bed. He was lying face down with one arm under him and the other turned back along side his body. I noticed that there was blood on his hand. It appeared from where I was standing that the blood was probably from defensive wounds to the hand. Whoever had killed him had not done a very clean job of it. It looked as if the victim might have heard his killer and tried to defend himself against an attack. I had to wonder if anyone might have heard it.

As I continued to look around from the doorway of the cabin, it became apparent to me that the room had been searched. The luggage was on the floor and everything that one might expect to find in that luggage was scattered about the cabin. That was something I would not have expected to find if it had been just a fight. Even the closet had everything pulled out and tossed around the cabin. It was easy to see why the Captain thought the motive was robbery. It certainly had all the earmarks of one.

I knelt down in the doorway to get a better look at the carpet. I started from the edge of the cabin and slowly worked my way toward the body. I could see where there had been blood tracked on the carpet from the body toward the door. It wasn't much, but it was enough for me to realize that someone had stepped in the victim's blood.

As I thought about it, I felt that finding bloody footprints didn't help much as it could have been the First Officer, the ship's steward, or even the ship's doctor. There was also the possibility that it was the killer's shoes that had made the bloody tracks in the carpet.

In order to eliminate whose shoeprints they were, I would want all of the shoes of those that I knew had been in the cabin to see if any of them had traces of blood on them. If none of those had blood on them, we were looking for a fourth person for sure. The fact that all three of the crew had been in the room would not be evidence enough that one of them had committed the crime. Any or all of them could have stepped in the victim's blood and left trace residue on their shoes.

"What are you looking for, Mr. McCord?"

The sound of Captain Klausen's voice disturbed my thoughts. I turned and looked at him. I had thought that he had taken the steward and the First Officer to the Officers' Mess

"Evidence, Captain," I said as I turned back and looked into the room. "I believe that there were at least four people in this room before I got here."

"How do you know that?"

"First of all, you told me about three of them. The other one was the killer. That is if the killer wasn't one of the three."

"Are you accusing one of the ship's crew of this crime?" he asked rather sharply.

I turned and looked at the Captain again before I commented. The look on his face indicated that he didn't like the idea that one of his crew might be responsible for the death of Mr. Wright.

"No, not yet. I'm simply trying to put it all together. Until I find out otherwise, everyone who has been in this cabin is a suspect."

"I see," he replied.

"Where is the ship's doctor?"

"I'm right here, Mr. McCord."

I turned and looked up to see a fairly tall middle-aged man in a uniform. He had dark brown eyes and wavy brown hair with a tinge of gray at the sideburns. I was sure that the women on board would find him rather handsome.

"Do you have some rubber gloves?"

"Yes, sir."

"Get me a pair and put on a pair yourself," I said. "I don't want to contaminate the crime scene any more than it already is."

I looked at the Captain. He seemed to be watching what we were doing, but I had other things I needed him to do.

"Captain, I need those statements," I reminded him.

"I'll go get started. I'll meet you in the Officers' Mess when you're finished here," the Captain said.

"It may be awhile," I assured him.

"Yes, of course," he replied then turned and walked down the passageway.

I glanced over at the Doctor. He was bent down next to his little black bag. He had his hand in it as he looked at me. The expression on his face gave me the impression that he wasn't sure who was running things.

The doctor seemed to gather his wits and retrieved two pair of rubber gloves from his bag. He handed me one pair. I continued to look at the crime scene as I put them on. Up to now I had not touched anything, but if I was going to examine the body and the room I would need them.

"I would like you to help me examine the body," I said as I stood up and checked to see that the doctor had gloves on.

"Yes, sir," he replied with a tone of reluctance in his voice.

I knelt down and pointed to the bloodstains on the carpet.

"Try not to step on the stains," I said as I stepped into the cabin.

I moved very carefully across the cabin toward the victim. Doctor Stillman followed along behind me. I knelt down next to the body and looked it over. There was a good deal of blood on the floor. I could not see any open wounds on the victim's back, his head, or any other part of his body that was visible to me which would account for the large amount of blood.

There was blood on his hands, which could have been from an effort to defend himself. Those wounds were obviously not serious enough to cause the large amount of blood that was on the floor close to the body.

As I looked at the body, I realized that the victim's head was in an unnatural position. It looked as if his neck may have been broken. The odd thing was that the position of the head was typical of someone who had been attacked from behind. It appeared as if his neck had been twisted sharply, snapping one or more of the cervical vertebras. That would certainly not account for the large amount of blood on the floor, either.

Doctor Stillman was kneeling beside me as I continued to examine the body. I was unable to find any gunshot wounds or knife wounds on the victim in his present position.

"I don't see anything on his back that would give cause for all this blood. Give me a hand. I want to roll him over," I said.

Together we rolled the body over on its side. It must have been a bit of a surprise to the doctor to see the handle of a knife sticking out of the man's chest as he suddenly took a deep breath.

"You okay?" I asked as I looked at him.

"Yes," he replied, but his voice did not seem to agree with the look on his face.

"Well, this explains the blood," I said as I looked around.

I examined the rest of the body to see if there was anything that I was missing. As I looked at the floor where the body had been lying, I discovered a small, delicate piece of jewelry. It was lying close to the man's pocket. I picked it up and examined it briefly. I had no idea what I had, but I knew someone who would.

"Do you have a safe place where we can put this?" I said as I held up the small piece of jewelry for the doctor to see.

"Yes. We can have it locked up in the Captain's safe."

"Do you have some plastic bags? Sandwich bags from the kitchen would do?"

"I don't have any with me, but I can get some from the galley," he replied looking at me as if he wondered why I would want sandwich bags.

"Go get them. I'll need several of them. I can use them for collecting evidence."

The expression on his face suddenly changed. It was as if he felt a little stupid for not thinking of that himself.

As soon as he left the cabin, I sat back on my heels and looked around some more. I had no idea what I was looking for, but I was sure I would know it when I saw it.

As my eyes scanned the cabin, I noticed the small safe was open. I moved closer to it in an effort to find out what was in it. I found out that there was nothing in the safe. There was no sign that anything had been in the safe except for the fact that it was wide open.

I turned around and again scanned the room from a little different angle. It was then that I saw something shiny sticking out from under the corner of the mattress. I carefully moved over to the edge of the bed. I lifted the mattress very carefully so as not to disturb anything. I discovered a silver brooch. It was about three to three and a half inches in diameter, and it appeared to be rather old. It was in perfect condition. There was something about it that made me feel like it was something I had seen before.

Since I was alone, I slipped the brooch into my pocket. I wanted Monica to get a good look at it before I turned it over to the Captain for safekeeping. I had no fear of losing fingerprints from it as the surface of the brooch was not smooth enough to have fingerprints that would be usable to identify anyone who had handled the brooch.

It was only a few minutes before Doctor Stillman returned. He had several plastic sandwich bags in his hand. He held one of them out to me. I dropped the small piece of jewelry that I had found while he was in the cabin in the bag and sealed it closed.

I then bent over the victim and carefully removed the knife from his chest taking care to note the angle of the knife in the body. I examined the knife before placing it in one of the bags. The knife was a common kitchen utility knife with about a five-inch long blade. It had been driven into the victim's chest with such force that it went in clear to the hilt.

"What do you think? Did the knife kill him, or was it the broken neck?" I asked the doctor.

Doctor Stillman looked at the body for a little while. It was clear that he was trying to figure out the cause of death.

"I'm not sure. Either one would most likely have killed him," he said after thinking about it for a moment.

"I agree, but my best guess, based on my years of experience as a homicide investigator, is that the snapping of the neck was what killed him. I would say that he was probably knifed first, but since that didn't kill him instantly, the killer snapped his neck. I can see no other possible reason to kill a man twice."

"I see your point," he replied, as he looked at me.

I again knelt down beside the body and began going through his pockets. I took his wallet out of his hip pocket and opened it. It contained several credit cards and a driver's license from the state of Illinois, but no cash. The fact that there was no cash in the victim's wallet seemed to support the theory that it was a robbery. The name on the credit cards and driver's license was that of William F. Lancaster of Calumet City, Illinois, a suburb of Chicago.

"What was the name of the person this cabin was registered to?" I asked the doctor.

"I believe I was told that it was registered to a Frank Wright from Chicago. Is that correct?"

"That's what I thought the Captain said. I think we better have a talk with the Captain and find out if Frank Wright and William Lancaster are one and the same, or if they are two different people."

"I think that would be a good idea," the doctor agreed.

I finished checking the body for anything else that might be important. We bagged everything in his pockets. We found nothing that one wouldn't expect to find in a man's pockets. There was certainly nothing in his pockets that I felt would be of help in the investigation at the moment. It was now up to the forensic lab people to find any additional evidence.

After locking the door to the cabin, Doctor Stillman and I took off our rubber gloves. I followed Doctor Stillman to the Officers' Mess.

CHAPTER FIVE

When Doctor Stillman and I finally arrived at the Officers' Mess, we found the ship's steward, the man who was supposed to have found the body, sitting at one of the tables. Captain Klausen was sitting across from him. I noticed a tape recorder on the table and it looked as if it was running. It appeared that they had been talking, but everything seemed to stop when we came in.

The First Officer was sitting at one of the other mess tables. He had his elbows on the table and his head in his hands. He looked like a man that was very upset over something, but that was easy to understand under the circumstances. I doubted that he was used to seeing dead people on the ship, especially ones that had died in such a violent and messy manner.

"How's it going?" I asked as I walked over to Captain Klausen.

"We have gone over every step of what happened as best as Steward James can remember," the Captain replied. "I hope that is what you wanted."

"Yes. That's fine," I replied.

"There is one thing that is bothering me," I said as I looked at the steward. "It was pretty late when you went to the victim's cabin. What were you doing at cabin two-sixty-one at such a late hour?"

The steward looked over at his captain before replying. When the captain nodded that he should answer, Steward James replied to my question.

"I went there to check on the man who was registered in that cabin," he replied, the expression on his face showing me no real concern.

"That would be Frank Wright?"

"Yes, sir," he replied.

He showed no expression of real concern for Mr. Wright. I got the feeling that there was something going on, but I had no idea what it might be.

"Are you sure that the body was that of Frank Wright?"

I got a funny look from the steward. It was as if he didn't know what I was talking about, or that it was a rather strange question to be asking.

"It was Mr. Wright, I'm sure of that."

"What makes you so sure?"

"I escorted him to his room when he came aboard. I saw his ticket, too. He didn't say anything when I called him by the name on the ticket."

I wasn't sure if the look on James's face was because he was confused by my questions, or if he wondered if I already knew that the victim might be someone else. I found his reaction not only puzzling, but also fascinating. I also found the detail of his answer interesting. Usually under such circumstances the details are not so well explained unless there is some underlining reason for detail. My question did not require such detail.

"Okay. I understand that you went to check on him, but what compelled you to go there in the first place?"

"I was directed by the First Officer to go and check on a complaint of unusual noise coming from that cabin."

"Do you know who called in to complain?"

"No, sir."

"What happened when you got to the cabin?"

"I knocked on the door, but no one answered."

"What did you do about that?" I asked as I looked him in the eyes.

"I went down the passageway and used the intercom to call the First Officer. I reported to him that I got no answer and that it was quiet now. He instructed me to open the door and check the cabin. He also told me that he was on his way down."

"If there was no answer and the room was quiet, why do you think he wanted you to check the cabin?"

"I don't know. I guess because he said that whoever reported the noise had said that it sounded like a fight was going on in the cabin."

The way he talked seemed almost as if he had rehearsed what he was going to say. His answers to my questions were a little too pat and a little too easily answered to suit me. There didn't seem to be any thought to them, no hesitation in answering them.

"Did he come right away?"

"Who?"

"The First Officer. Did he come to the cabin right away?"

"He got there only a few minutes after I found the - - the - - body," he said, his voice suddenly showing how upset he still was over it.

The way he said it gave me the impression that he wasn't as upset over seeing the victim as he would have liked me to believe. I felt his sudden show of being upset after he had been answering the rest of my questions without any emotion was phony.

"Did you see anyone in the passageways on your way to the cabin?"

"No, sir."

"No one? A passenger, a fellow crew member, no one?"

"No, sir. I saw no one," he insisted.

"Did you hear anything while you were in the passageway? Maybe someone talking in a nearby cabin, or possibly someone was closing a door somewhere down the passageway?" I asked, as I continued to look him in the eyes.

"Nothing. It's pretty quiet on the ship at that hour, sir," the steward added.

The emphasis on "sir" at the end of his sentence led me to believe that he was getting a little upset with me. I had to wonder why. I had not been badgering him and I doubted that the captain had been.

I looked at the steward as I thought about what he had said. The fact was, I was more interested in the way he said it than I was in what he said. The question that came to my mind was is he telling me everything he could remember, or was he holding something back from me? I noticed that he would look from me to the Captain, and sometimes across the room toward the First Officer. Why was he so concerned about the First Officer? I could understand his concern with the Captain. After all he was his boss. But why the First Officer? What possible reason could there be for his interest in the First Officer, unless he was afraid that the First Officer would tell a different story.

As I thought about the steward and the First Officer, I had to wonder how long they had been in the victim's cabin before they notified the Captain. It would also be interesting to know if the steward had been in the cabin before the First Officer got there, and for how long. Another question was how long did it take for the Captain to get to the cabin.

I glanced over at the First Officer. He looked pretty shaken by all this, much more so than the steward. I had to wonder if the First Officer could have managed to search the victim's cabin before he called for help. There was something about the way the First Officer looked that gave me the impression that he was not capable of searching and stealing anything from the victim's cabin, especially with the victim lying there on the floor in a pool of blood. It might have been his pale, almost ashen, complexion that led me to believe he was truly upset over what he had seen in the cabin.

I certainly didn't have the same feelings about the steward. His behavior led me to believe that he may have been around a bit more than he would like me to believe. His demeanor when I questioned him caused me to think that he had been talked to by authorities before, and not once but possibly several times.

I wasn't ready to say he was a hardened criminal, but there was something about the way he handled himself when questioned that caused me to think that he knew how the Justice System worked, and not from the outside. I had questioned too many men over the years as a police officer not to pick up on the little things that told me when they were not telling me the truth. The problem I often had was trying to determine what part was the truth and what part was a lie. They often tended to mix the two together making it more difficult to get to the truth.

The steward was guilty of something, but I didn't know what it might be. I didn't think that he had killed the man. He didn't impress me as the type. A check into the steward's background might prove interesting. I would have to talk to the Captain about it later. I decided that I would not question the steward any more, at least not right now.

"If you're done with your statement, you can return to your duties," I said to the steward. "If you think of anything else, please let us know."

He didn't comment on my statement. He simply looked from me to the Captain. When the Captain nodded that he could go, the steward smiled slightly, then stood up and left the Officers' Mess.

"I would like to talk to the First Officer, now," I said to the Captain.

"Certainly. I have his statement already."

"Good. I'll listen to it later. I want to talk to him now."

"Certainly."

I got up and walked across the room to where the First Officer was sitting. As I sat down across the table from him, he looked up at me. The look in his eyes gave me a clue as to what was going on in his head. He appeared to still be rather shaken by what he had seen.

"I'm Nick McCord. What's your name?"

"First Officer Dunbar, sir. William Dunbar.

"How are you doing, William?" I asked.

"Not so well. I've never seen anything like that before," he said, his voice cracking slightly as he talked.

"I'm sure you haven't, but I have a few questions I need to ask you. Do you think you could answer a few more questions for me?"

"Yes, sir."

"Who called you to complain about the unusual noise in cabin two-sixty-one?"

"I don't really know."

"You don't know?"

"No, sir. The person wouldn't give his name. I asked, but he wouldn't tell me," he said as if he didn't think I believed him.

"You said 'he'. Was the person who called a man?"

"Yes, sir. I think so."

"But you're not sure?"

"I'm pretty sure it was a man."

"Did you happen to recognize the voice, or did it seem at all familiar?"

"No, sir," he replied shaking his head.

"Did the person call from one of the cabins?"

"No, sir. The call was made from one of the passageway intercom phones."

"You're saying that the call was not made from one of the cabins?"

"That's right. Anyone can use the passageway phones," he said. "They're supposed to be used by the crew for emergencies only, but sometimes passengers use them to report things to the bridge."

"So what you're saying is that anyone on board could have called you to report the noise from anywhere on the ship?"

"Well, yes and no."

"What do you mean by that? Explain yourself."

"There's a panel on the bridge that lights up to tell us which intercom phone is being used. That way we can tell where that person is calling from, you know, from what part of the ship. The complaint was called in from an intercom phone located on Deck Two only a couple of doors down the passageway from cabin two-sixty-one."

"So you can tell where a call on the intercom is made from?"

"Yes, sir," he replied.

I turned and looked at the Captain. He didn't say anything, but I got the feeling that he knew what I was thinking. I turned back to the First Officer.

"Do you know where James was when you got the complaint about the unusual noise?"

"No, not exactly. He would have to have been on Deck Three near the lounge as that is where he answered the intercom."

"James answered the intercom on Deck Three, and the call came in from the intercom on Deck Two, is that right?"

"Yes, sir," the First Officer replied looking a bit puzzled by my question.

I had to think about what he was telling me. It seemed that it might have been difficult for James to get from Deck Two near the front of the ship to Deck Three that was closer to the rear.

"About how long did it take you to get hold of James?"

"From the time I got the complaint until I was able to get hold of James was maybe, ah, six to seven minutes, I would guess. I don't think it would have been any longer then that," he said thoughtfully.

I wasn't sure, but if I had to guess, I might be able to make from cabin two-sixty-one to the lounge area in that amount of time especially since it was late and the passageways would most likely be empty. That was one thing I would have to check out.

"One more thing, do you happen to know where James was prior to receiving the complaint over the intercom phone?"

"No, sir. Not really," he replied.

"Prior to the complaint, when was the last time you saw James or spoke to him?" I asked.

"Let me think," he said as he leaned back in the chair.

I watched him as he took a moment to think.

"It would have been at least an hour, maybe a little more. No, it was closer to two hours. He came up on the bridge and brought coffee for the helmsman and me."

"Where do you spend your time when you are on watch?"

"I spend most of my time on the bridge unless there's a problem that I have to deal with."

"Were there any other problems last night?"

"No, sir. Everything was running smoothly."

"Then you spent the entire evening on the bridge until you went down to cabin two-sixty-one? Is that right?"

"Yes, sir. Well, except for the few minutes when I went to the head."

"When was that?"

"You mean, when did I go to the head?" he asked.

"Yes."

"I don't know, maybe about fifteen or twenty minutes before the steward brought up coffee. I remember because when I returned to the bridge, the helmsmen told me that he had sent down for some coffee."

"Does it normally take that long to get coffee to the bridge?"

"Sometimes, but not normally."

At the moment I could think of nothing else to ask him that would put me any closer to the answers I needed. I decided that I would let this witness return to his duties, but I would most likely be talking to him again.

"I have nothing further to ask you at this time. If you think of anything at all that might assist us in this, please let the Captain know," I said as I looked at him.

"Yes, sir."

First Officer Dunbar looked over at the Captain. When the Captain nodded that it was all right for him to return to his duties, First Officer Dunbar stood up, nodded at me, then turned and left the Officers' Mess.

Captain Klausen and I watched as the First Officer left the Officers' Mess. I wasn't sure what to think, but his answers seemed logical. I then turned to the Captain.

"Well, Mr. McCord, what do you think?"

"I think your steward is not telling me all he knows."

"You think he killed that man?" the Captain asked with a surprised look on his face.

"No. I don't think so. I think he might have done a little ransacking of the room to see if there was anything of value that he could steal and possibly sell later. He would have had time before he called the First Officer. He may have even stolen something from the room, but I don't think he killed anyone," I said as I thought about the steward.

"I would like to see a background check on him, and on William F. Lancaster and Frank Wright. I've got a feeling that Frank Wright does not exist, at least not on this ship."

"I'll get a message out tonight. Anything else?"

"Yes, I want that cabin sealed off until it can be gone over by the Coast Guard and their forensic people. I believe that they are the ruling authority in a situation like this?"

"That is correct. We are currently in U.S. waters so they would be. I have already gotten a call off to them. They will meet us at Mackinac Island before we dock," Captain Klausen said.

"By the way, I think you should make sure that your steward does not get off the ship when we dock. If he did find something of value in that room, or if he's scared and thinks that he might get blamed for the killing, there's a possibility that he might try to run."

"I'll tend to it," the Captain replied.

"I'm going to go get some rest. I'll see you in the morning, or should I say, I'll see you later."

"It is rather late, Mr. McCord. I do want to thank you for your assistance. I'm sure that the cruise line will be more than willing to compensate you for your time and effort. And I'm sure the Coast Guard will be glad that you were here to help out."

"We'll see about that. Goodnight, Captain," I said with a smile to acknowledge his compliment.

As I walked back to my suite, I began to wonder how much the Coast Guard would appreciate my efforts to help find out who had committed the murder aboard the ship. I had no idea how much experience they would have in this kind of an investigation, but I was sure that I would soon find out.

I hoped that they would not focus their entire investigation on the steward, but I was sure that they would be taking a hard look at him. They should make an effort to screen the entire passenger list before letting anyone off the ship.

My gut feeling still told me that the steward did not kill Mr. Lancaster, or whoever he was. If that was the case, there had to be someone else aboard the ship that did kill him.

* * * *

When I got to our suite, I found Monica lying on the bed sound asleep. She was dressed as if she had expected me to return much sooner than I did. It was apparent that she had been unable to keep her eyes open. I know mine were ready to close as soon as I laid down.

I tried to lie down on the bed as quietly as possible in the hope of not waking her. As I lowered myself onto the bed, she opened her eyes and rolled over toward me.

"You're back. What took you so long?"

"This one is not going to be easy. It was pretty messy."

"Any suspects?"

"Yeah, two known and at least one unknown."

"What do you mean?"

"The ship's steward and the First Officer are the known. If it wasn't one of them, then I have no idea who did it."

"Any idea what the motive might be?" she asked as she raised her head up and supported it with her hand.

"It looks like it may have been robbery. I found a couple of pieces of jewelry that look to be rather old and may be worth a lot of money."

"Will I be able to see the jewelry?" she asked rather excitedly.

"Sure. I've got one piece with me," I said as I reached into my pocket and pulled it out.

Monica took the silver brooch, swung her legs over the side of the bed and sat up. I watched her as she turned on the light beside the bed. She turned the brooch over and over in her hand as she carefully examined it.

"Oh, my God," she said almost under her breath.

"What is it?" I asked as I swung my legs over the side of the bed and moved around beside her.

Monica turned her head and looked at me, but didn't say anything. The look on her face caused me to worry.

"What is it?" I asked again.

"I'm not one hundred percent sure, but this looks like a piece of the jewelry that we found at Tom's Lodge," the sound of her voice showing how surprised she was to see the brooch.

"What? You mean it is from Gill's Point Lodge?"

It was not that I didn't understand what she was saying. It was that I couldn't believe what it meant. If she was right, we were dealing with jewelry that had been stolen from ships on the Great Lakes over a hundred years ago by a man named Bartholomew Samuelson. Captain Samuelson had pirated valuables from ships on the Great Lakes and stored them in an old copper mine at his large home on the shore of Lake Michigan. It was that home Tom Walker had purchased a hundred years later and turned it into Gill's Point Lodge near Gill's Rock, Wisconsin.

After it became a lodge, relatives of Captain Samuelson went to the lodge, searched the lodge and it grounds. They found the mine where the treasure was stored. In the process of removing the treasure from the mine, three of the four people involved in removing the treasure died. The one that survived, I caught and he went to jail for murdering one of the others.

I looked from Monica's face to the brooch, then back at Monica. I didn't know what to say. All I could think about was how did it get on board the ship, and how did Mr. Lancaster get his hands on it? The only possible answer I could think of was that it had been stolen from the museum where it had been sent and then brought aboard the ship.

"It's the same kind of jewelry and dates from about the same period as the jewelry we found there," Monica added. "I'm almost sure this is one of the pieces that I examined before it was sent out to a museum."

"Do you know which museum this piece went to?"

"No, but it shouldn't be too difficult to find out. Each museum should have an inventory list of what they received."

"There's nothing we can do right now. I think we should try to get some sleep and see what we can find out in the morning."

"Good idea. What should I do with this brooch?"

"We'll need to hide it. I would suspect that the Coast Guard will be searching the entire ship in the morning."

"Even our suite?" she asked.

"It's possible. Just in case, we'd better hide it well."

We looked around the place until we found a good place to hide the brooch. We pinned it to a small piece of fabric on the underside of a chair. I pinned it in such a way that if the chair was turned over, it still would be very difficult to see, if not impossible. The only way to see it would be to pull the piece of fabric away from the bottom of the chair.

We laid back down on the bed to get some rest. I know it took Monica a long time to finally go back to sleep. It took me a little longer as my mind was filled with the events of the evening.

CHAPTER SIX

For the second time in the same night, I was awakened by the sound of someone knocking on my door. It was a rude awakening to me as I felt as if I had hardly gotten any sleep at all. I swung my legs over the side of the bed and looked over my shoulder at Monica. She was still in her clothes from last night, as was I.

"Who could that be now," she asked, obviously not pleased that we had been awakened, again.

"Don't know," I replied as I stood up.

I walked to the door and looked out through the peephole. There were three men standing outside the door to our suite. One looked like he might be an officer while the other two looked like Coast Guardsmen.

I unlocked the door and opened it. The man standing right in front of me was a young Coast Guard Ensign.

"Are you Mr. Nicholas McCord?"

"Yes," I replied as I began to wonder what had happened now.

"Commander Stivers of the United States Coast Guard would like to see you in the Officers' Mess, sir," the young Ensign said without any emotion in his voice and a stern serious look on his face.

"Tell your Commander Stivers that I'll be there in a few minutes."

"He wants us to escort you, now, sir."

"I don't need an escort, Ensign. I will be there as soon as I clean up," I said, the tone of my voice making it clear that I would not be rushed. "But if you feel the need to wait for me, I'll be with you in a few minutes."

I closed the door in his face without giving him a chance to respond. I figured that he had been instructed to bring me to the Officers' Mess and that he would still be standing there when I was ready.

"What's going on?" Monica asked.

"It seems the Coast Guard has arrived. They want me in the Officers' Mess."

"Will they be the lead agency investigating the murder?"

"That would be my guess. Anyway, I want you to come with me," I said as I went into the bathroom.

Monica changed her clothes and combed her hair. I changed clothes while she was in the bathroom. When we were ready to follow the Ensign to the Officers' Mess, we went to the door. I stopped and looked at her. Even with little sleep, she was a fantastic looking woman.

"I think we better take that brooch with us. It might convince the Commander that we know what we're doing, and about the motive for the murder."

I turned around, went to the chair, tipped it over and unpinned the brooch. As I put it in my pocket, I returned to Monica's side and then opened the door. We found the Ensign and the two Coast Guardsmen waiting for us.

"I'm ready," I said with a smile.

"The Commander wishes to see just you, sir," the Ensign said.

"Sorry, Ensign, but Doctor Barnhart is an expert in certain matters related to this crime. They will become very clear to your Commander once he talks to her. She is key to this investigation, and she is coming with me whether you like it or not," I said, giving the Ensign no real choice unless he wanted to make a scene, which I seriously doubted.

"Yes, sir," he finally conceded.

I smiled, and then we turned down the passageway and walked toward the stairway that would take us to the deck where the Officers' Mess was located. I could hear the footsteps of the Ensign and the two Coast Guardsmen behind us.

As we walked, Monica reached over and casually took hold of my hand. I couldn't even guess what was going through her mind, but I could feel her nervousness through her hand. I guess I couldn't blame her as I was a little nervous, too. I was about to have to deal with the U.S. Coast Guard, a group I was unfamiliar with and knew little about their policies and procedures. The only thing I knew was that they operated like no police department I had worked with before. I had no idea what to expect from them.

* * * *

As we entered the Officers' Mess, I noticed a rather pleasant looking man wearing the uniform of the United States Coast Guard. The three gold stripes on the sleeves of his jacket told me that he was a Commander. There was also Captain Klausen and First Officer Dunbar in the room. They all stood up as we entered the room with the Ensign right behind us. When I glanced over my shoulder at the Ensign, I noticed that the Coast Guardsmen were no longer there. I was sure that they were probably posted outside the door.

"Good morning, Mr. McCord. I'm Commander Stivers."

"Good morning, Commander. This is Monica Barnhart."

"It is very nice to meet you," Commander Stivers said politely. "Although I'm pleased to meet you, Miss Barnhart, I don't think your attendance at this meeting will be necessary, and might prove to be rather distressing for you."

It was clear that Monica did not appreciate his apparent chauvinistic attitude toward her. I was about to say something when Monica spoke.

"First of all, it's Doctor Barnhart. I already know what this meeting is about, Commander, and I agree with you that it is rather distressing. However, you might find that I have information that could be of some interest to you. But, if you prefer, I will be glad to return to my suite and let you figure it out for yourself," she said then waited for him to respond.

The look on the Commander's face was priceless. He stood there with his mouth hanging open for a moment. He looked at Captain Klausen as if he were looking to him for something to say. There was no doubt in my mind that the Commander had not been put down with such class in a very long time, if ever. Even though he deserved the put down, I felt it was time to step in and put things in their proper perspective, and maybe even make the Commander feel a little more at ease.

"Commander, Doctor Barnhart is not only a first rate investigator, she is an expert on antique jewelry. And antique jewelry is what this murder is all about."

The Commander looked at me for a moment, before he said anything.

"What are you saying, Mr. McCord?"

"At Captain Klausen's request, I took a look at the crime scene last night, or should I say early this morning."

"He had no right to let you do that," Commander Stivers said.

"Maybe not, but without my help there is no telling how much of the evidence in that cabin would have been destroyed."

"Commander," Captain Klausen interrupted, "Mr. McCord is a former homicide detective on the Milwaukee Police Department. He is very well known in the law enforcement community across the country as an expert in the collecting of evidence and preservation of a crime scene. I felt his expertise would be most valuable under the circumstances."

"How is it that you know so much about Mr. McCord?" Commander Stivers asked.

"I've read a lot about him when he broke up a plan to steal large amounts of jewelry that had been pirated on the

Great Lakes. The crime of piracy happened over a hundred years ago."

"Well, it seems that we should look to you to help us in this matter," Commander Stivers said, the tone of his voice causing me to wonder if he was being sarcastic, condescending, or if he really meant it. "What can you tell me about this murder?"

"Two pieces of antique jewelry were found at the scene," I said.

"Two?" Captain Klausen asked with surprise.

"Yes, two. The one I gave to you for safekeeping, and the one I kept for Doctor Barnhart to closely inspect without any distractions," I said as I pulled the brooch out of my pocket and handed it to Commander Stivers.

The Commander looked at the brooch for a minute then looked up at me, then at Monica.

"You needn't worry about fingerprints. That brooch would not reveal any as the surface is too irregular to provide any usable prints," I explained to the Commander.

"The brooch that you hold in your hand was part of the treasure that was discovered in a lodge near Gill's Rock, Wisconsin. This is where Doctor Barnhart comes in," I said as I looked over to Monica.

"Some of the jewelry from the lodge was claimed by relatives that could prove it had belonged to a family member who had disappeared on the Great Lakes. While some remained on display at the lodge, most of it was sent to several museums, most of them in Wisconsin and Illinois," Monica explained.

"How did this brooch get aboard this ship?" Commander Stivers asked.

"That we haven't figured out," I admitted.

"We need to check with the museums that received some of the jewelry and find out if any of it is missing. I'm sure that none of the jewelry that was left at the lodge is missing or Tom would have told us," Monica said.

"Who is this Tom fella?" Commander Stivers asked.

"Tom Walker. He is the owner of the lodge where some of the jewelry was kept. He is also a good friend of mine," I said.

"He is aboard this ship, by the way," Captain Klausen added.

"Anyway, we also need to find out who the victim really is as we have two identities, the one in his wallet and the one he used when he registered aboard this ship," I said.

"What's your best guess as to what happened, Mr. McCord?"

"My guess is that the victim, and at least one other person, stole the jewelry and brought it aboard the ship. I suspect that they were using the ship as a means of escape."

"Using this ship as a means of escape doesn't seem logical to me," Captain Stivers said looking at me as if I didn't know very much about criminals.

"If you think about it, you might look at it a little differently. We are not dealing with amateurs here. I'm sure they would know that other means of travel would most likely be watched. They probably felt that a cruise ship would not be watched as closely as it is a rather slow way to get anywhere.

"The most likely scenario is that those involved in the theft of the jewelry had some kind of a falling out. Probably one of them got a little greedy and tried to take an extra piece or two of the jewelry for himself. They fought over it, and one of them killed the other. The murderer then took all the jewelry except for the two pieces that we found. The brooch that I found under the edge of the mattress, and the small pin Doctor Stillman and I found under the victim's body when we turned him over. In the murderer's haste to get out of the room, he probably didn't even miss them, or he didn't feel he had time to look for them."

"You think it's that simple?" Commander Stivers asked.

"Frankly, it's never that simple. That is a simplified summary of what I think might have happened. But based on the fact that we only found two pieces of jewelry, one of them hidden under the mattress, might suggest that one of the thieves was trying to hide a couple of pieces so he got a little bigger share of the loot. Greed tends to make for problems even among thieves.

"I came to that conclusion because there was a safe in the cabin. Why hide something under the mattress when it would easily fit in the safe if all you wanted to do was make sure it wasn't stolen?"

"I see your point. But you got all that from what little you saw in the room?" Commander Stivers asked.

The look on the Commander's face indicating that he wasn't sure I knew what I was talking about.

"That, and a lot more, Commander."

"A lot more? How do you know that there was more jewelry? Isn't it all speculation on your part?"

"Yes. And I don't know for sure if there was more jewelry. But remember Doctor Barnhart and I have seen that jewelry before. The two pieces that we found are part of a much bigger collection. I can't see anyone killing over just the two pieces we found. In and of themselves, the two pieces we found are worth maybe - - - ," I said, then looked to Monica for a little help.

"They are worth maybe six to seven hundred dollars," Monica said.

"Six or seven hundred dollars?" Commander Stivers asked.

"Yes. By the way, each is worth about that much," Monica added.

"That seems to me to be worth the effort to find," Commander Stivers said. "I've heard of people killing for a lot less than that."

"I have as well," I replied. "But you have to remember these pieces are not the kind of jewelry a petty thief would take. This is the kind of jewelry that only big time thieves go after. Let me explain."

"Please do."

"First of all, it requires a reasonably good knowledge of the value of the jewelry. Then you have to have someone on the other end that is willing to pay for these rare pieces. A small time thief would not normally have the necessary connections to dispose of it quickly, nor would he likely know the value of what he stole."

"What makes you think that there were more than just the two pieces that you found?"

"The in-cabin safe was open and empty. The fact that the safe was open would indicate that there had been something in it, probably more jewelry," I explained. "The in-cabin safes are normally closed until the passenger opens them to use."

"There's also the fact that the jewelry found in the room had been sent to a museum along with a good number of other pieces. None of the museums received less than ten pieces, while a couple of the larger museums received a lot more. At least a couple of the larger museums received close to a hundred pieces, each," Monica added.

"Now that doesn't mean that there was more, but I did see what looked to be bloody finger prints on the door of the safe. That would indicate that someone at least looked into the safe after the victim was killed. Why would you look in the safe unless you expected to find something of value in it?" I asked.

"I see what you mean. You said that you found more in the room. What else did you find?"

"There were other people in the room after the victim was murdered, at least three. Four if you wish to count me", I added.

"Three? Do you know who they are?"

"Yes. Doctor Stillman, First Officer Dunbar and the steward. I believe the steward's name is James."

"That is correct," Captain Klausen confirmed. "By the way, Mr. McCord, I have asked for a check into James's background as you requested."

"Thank you," I replied.

"You requested a background check on this James fella? Why? Do you think he might be the killer?" Commander Stivers asked.

"No. I don't think he killed the victim."

"Then why the background check?"

"I think he might have ransacked the cabin after the murder."

Commander Stivers looked at me for a moment as if he were trying to understand what I was getting at. From the look on his face it was clear that he couldn't see where I was coming from. I thought it might be a good idea to clear things up for him.

"Let me explain," I said in an effort to relieve his curiosity.

"Please do."

"I don't see James doing the killing. It was a very messy job. There was also very strong evidence that a struggle had taken place in the cabin, not somewhere else. James is a fairly small man and doesn't appear to be very strong. The victim, on the other hand, was a good size man, over six feet tall, and appeared to be in good physical shape.

"James strikes me as more of a small time thief, not likely to get into a physical confrontation with someone who is obviously much bigger and stronger than he is. Also, from the way the victim was killed, James would have been a mess. He would have had blood all over him and his uniform, and probably several cuts or bruises on his person. I seriously doubt that James would have had time to clean up based on the timetable we were able to establish. Beside, from my experience, James is probably a petty crook."

"What gives you that idea?"

"From my talk with him last night, it would be my guess that he has been in trouble with the law before, but nothing like this. Maybe petty theft, but certainly nothing this serious."

"So you're saying that he ransacked the room after the murder?" Commander Stivers asked.

"That would be my guess, but I could be wrong. If I'm right about him having a police record, once we have his record we can probably put a little pressure on him. He might tell us what he saw in the cabin before he ransacked it, especially if he thinks he might go to jail for murder."

"Where do we go from here?" Commander Stivers asked, the tone of his voice far more pleasant and more willing to listen to me.

"We need to go over the cabin with a fine tooth comb. We need to get blood and hair samples, and check for fingerprints in the cabin. We need to have an autopsy done on the victim to see what he can tell us. And we need to find out where they got hold of the jewelry. We also need to find out who the victim really is."

"I'll have a forensic team meet the ship at Mackinac Island. They can go over the cabin there and fly any evidence they find to our labs in Chicago or Detroit for immediate evaluation," Commander Stivers said.

"That sounds good," I agreed.

"What about our landing at Mackinac Island? What will I tell our passengers?" Captain Klausen asked.

"You'll have to keep them on board while we interview them," Commander Stivers said.

"Excuse me, Commander, but Mackinac Island is just that, an island. Captain, if you gave a list of the passengers to the Coast Guard, and they put men at each of the docks so no one could leave on another boat; it might force the killer back on the boat," I suggested.

"What would that accomplish, Mr. McCord?" Captain Klausen asked."

"First of all, it would give us time. Time to figure out who the killer might be and what his plans are. I would, however, restrict James to the ship. If he thinks that he is a suspect, he might try to run."

I could see that Commander Stivers was thinking over what I had suggested.

"There is always the chance that our killer might escape by getting off the ship on the island and not returning. But my guess is that he would not want to draw that kind of attention to himself, not with all that is at stake for him.

"Our killer is not stupid," I reminded the Commander. "He would have to know that anyone that didn't return to the ship would quickly become a suspect. He would have to know that both the United States and Canada would be looking for him. That would certainly limit his ability to get to wherever it is he is planning on going."

"Do you really think our killer is that smart?"

"Yes. Yes, I do," I replied after giving it some thought. "You can't just walk into a museum and steal a bunch of jewelry and walk out with it. It takes planning. He put a great deal of time and effort into this. He is not going to do anything to cast suspicion on himself at this point. If he planned to get off the ship at a certain place, he most likely will not change those plans. To get off the ship anywhere but where his ticket was for would bring immediate attention to him. I doubt he wants that, at least until he gets to where he is going," I explained.

"It is my understanding that none of the tickets end here. Am I correct?" I asked of Captain Klausen.

"That is correct," Captain Klausen replied.

"There is an airport on the island," Commander Stivers reminded me.

"Yes, I know. But there are very few flights out of there. It should be pretty easy to watch," I suggested.

"We could do that," Commander Stivers agreed.

"Can we get everyone in place by the time we dock at the island?" I asked.

"Yes. I'll get right on it. We have a Coast Guard station on the island. I can have extra personnel there in minutes."

"Good. I think it would be a good idea if we keep as much of this to ourselves as possible," I suggested. "There is no need to let every passenger know what has happened here."

"I'm sure the shipping company would appreciate that," Captain Klausen said.

"Good, then we're all in agreement?" I asked as I looked from Captain Klausen to Commander Stivers.

Once we had all agreed to keep it quiet, Monica and I left the Officers' Mess and returned to our suite. We got ready to go get something to eat.

CHAPTER SEVEN

We were about ready to leave our suite and go to the restaurant for brunch when we heard a knock on the door. I looked at Monica. The expression on her face was that of "not again". I was sure she was getting tired of people knocking on our door at all hours. I know I was.

I got up from the loveseat and went to the door. I glared through the peephole and saw that it was Tom and Pamela.

"It's Tom and Pamela," I said as I looked back at Monica.

"What are you going to say to them?"

"Beats me, but if I don't answer the door they'll know something is wrong."

I reached out and opened it. I could see by the look on Tom's face that he had something on his mind. The expression on his face reminded me of a little boy who had seen his first airplane take off.

"Have you looked out the window," Tom said, his voice showing how excited he was.

"Good morning, Tom. Good morning, Pamela," I said ignoring him as I stepped back to let them come in.

"Good morning, Nick," Pamela said with a grin.

"Morning. Haven't you looked outside?" Tom asked.

"No, not really. What is it, Tom?"

"There's a Coast Guard Cutter cruising along side us."

"So? The Coast Guard does patrol the Great Lakes," I reminded him.

"Yes, I know. But we watched them. They moved up along side. They had some men on board this ship. We saw several men in a launch going from this ship back to the cutter. The men were in uniforms and were armed to the teeth. It was like one of those Coast Guard boarding parties you see in the movies."

It was hard for me to keep from smiling at Tom's excitement. I think it would have been almost amusing if the reason for the Coast Guard's men being on board had been different.

"I know," I said casually."

"You know?" Tom asked with a surprised tone in his voice. "If you know, tell me what's going on?"

"I think it would be a good idea if they sat down for this," Monica suggested looking up at me from the loveseat.

Pamela looked at Monica. The expression on her face indicated that she wasn't sure if she was ready to hear about what was happening. She glanced over at me before moving across the room and sitting down on one of the chairs in the sitting area next to Monica.

The look on Tom's face was priceless. I got the impression that he wasn't sure if he should believe anything I was going to tell him. But he wasn't about to leave and miss out on one single word about it, either.

"Has something happened that may cause the ship to sink, or have they come to get a passenger off the ship," Pamela asked Monica with a very concerned look on her face.

"No to both questions. Nothing like that. The ship is fine," Monica assured her.

"Okay, Nick. What do you mean, you know? Come on, tell us," Tom said with a grin as if he were expecting some wild tale.

"I guess there is no other way to say this, but to simply tell you. I think you should both know that there has been a murder on board the ship," I said, the tone of my voice hopefully leaving no room for doubt about my sincerity.

"A murder! Aboard this ship?" Pamela blurted out.

Her eyes were as big as saucers and her mouth hung open. I wasn't sure if she was going into shock, or having a panic attack.

"Yes, a murder."

"On this ship?"

"Yes, Pamela. On this ship. It happened last night," Monica said softly and calmly. "But it has nothing to do with any of us."

I knew that Monica was trying to settle Pamela's suddenly frayed nerves. We both knew that it had everything to do with us, at least Monica and me. We were already into it up to our necks. We knew that now that we were involved in the investigation, nothing was sacred. If the killer thought that we were helping to trap him, he could turn on us as quickly as a rattlesnake. The fact that he had killed once only made it that much more serious.

"Who was killed? One of the passengers?" Tom asked.

"Yes. We don't know what his name is, yet. But we will before long," I replied.

"Have you figured out why he was killed?"

"We think it was most likely robbery."

"Robbery?" Tom said as he shook his head in disbelief. "That's ridiculous. That's the dumbest thing I've heard of in a long time. How could anyone expect to get away with robbery on a ship? Certainly the killer must realize that there is no place to go except for a swim, and I doubt that he is that good a swimmer. It wouldn't be any big thing for the Coast Guard to come aboard and search every inch of this ship."

Then I noticed Tom's eyes light up as if he had a brilliant idea. A grin slowly came over his face.

"That's why the Coast Guard was here, to search the ship. Wasn't it?"

"No. Not really. They are here to investigate a homicide, the robbery was secondary."

Tom looked at me as if he didn't understand what I had said.

"What do you mean?"

"Tom, do you remember the incident that took place at your lodge a while back?"

"You mean when you and Monica were at the lodge?" he asked, the expression on his face suddenly turning serious as he started to wonder what I was getting at.

"Yes."

"Yeah, sure. I could never forget that. But what does that have to do with this?"

"It seems that some of the same jewelry that was found at your lodge has turned up on this ship."

Tom looked at me in disbelief.

"You're kidding. Right?"

"No. I'm not."

Tom's face began to turn pale and his eyes showed how hard it was for him to believe that it could be happening all over again. His head slowly tipped down as he put his hands over his face and leaned forward resting his elbows on his knees. His breathing became shallow as he stared blankly at the floor.

"Not again," Tom said in a long sigh that was so soft it was hard to hear.

Tom shook his head in disbelief.

I glanced over at Pamela. She was looking at Tom. I don't know what she was thinking, but from the look on her face she was very confused. It was clear that she was trying to figure out what Tom could possibly have to do with any of this, especially a robbery and a murder. She turned and looked at me as if she was looking for me to explain what was going on.

"Are you saying that Tom is involved in the murder of one of the passengers?" Pamela asked, her face showing that she was having a hard time understanding any of what we were saying.

"No," I said. "He is not involved."

"You're his friend. You know he couldn't do such a thing. Besides, he couldn't have done it. He was with me all night last night," she blurted out.

The expression on Pamela's face suddenly changed. She had apparently not wanted anyone to know that they had spent the night together. She looked a little embarrassed as she glanced from me to Monica and then to Tom.

"It's okay," Monica said softly.

Monica assured her as she put her arm around Pamela in an effort to reassure her that everything was going to be all right.

"Tom is not a suspect in the murder, or the robbery. He doesn't need an alibi," Monica added.

"No. Tom is not a suspect," I assured her.

Tom raised his head and looked at me for a moment before he spoke.

"Are you sure that the jewelry that was found at my lodge is the same jewelry that was found here, on this ship?" Tom asked, apparently finding it hard to believe.

"Yes," Monica replied. "I personally examined the two pieces that were found here. However, it was not any of the pieces that are on display at your lodge. It was some of the jewelry that was sent out to the museums."

"All I can say is that jewelry really gets around," he said as he looked at Pamela. "It was stolen over a hundred years ago on the Great Lakes. And now it shows up again on a ship on the Great Lakes. Plus, it has apparently been stolen again.

"What do you think happened this time?" Tom asked as turned and looked to me for answers.

"We think that it was stolen from one of the museums and brought aboard the ship by the thieves."

"You said "thieves". Does that mean you think there was more than one?"

"Yes. Now mind you, this is all a theory, and only a theory. It may not have been played out this way at all. We are not sure what happened, or the order in which it may have happened. We think the thieves stole the jewelry from one or more museums and brought it aboard the ship. After they got aboard the ship, and probably after we got under way, they had some sort of a falling out. Maybe one of them got a little greedy and wanted it all, or maybe they couldn't agree on the split, who knows. It could have been any number of things.

"Anyway, we believe that one of the thieves killed the other and took all the loot except for the two pieces that we found," I explained.

"So you think the killer and the victim were in it together?" Tom asked.

"Yes, we do. The only problem is that we don't know how many are involved, or where they're headed. There could have been three or more involved for all we know."

"You said that they took all the loot except for the two pieces that you found. Does that mean you think there is a lot more?" Pamela asked.

"We're not sure; but, yes, we think so. The two pieces we found were part of a much larger cache of jewelry. If they were able to get their hands on the two pieces, it only seems logical that they would have been able to steal all of it, or at least more than what we found," I explained.

"The two pieces alone would not be worth much compared to the entire collection at one of the museums. The collection at one museum runs somewhere between eight hundred and fifty thousand dollars to just under a million dollars," Monica added. "More if they got more than just one museum's part of the complete collection."

"What was the complete collection worth?" Pamela asked.

"The complete collection which included more than just jewelry was worth close to six million dollars, but the collection was broken up because it was so big that one museum could not display or even store it all. There was enough jewelry, silverware, and other valuables that it could be spread out to several museums located around the Great Lakes so that more people could see it. Most of the jewelry was sent to two primary museums."

"Do you know where those two pieces you found came from?" Pamela asked.

"Not yet, but we're checking on it. At the time the jewelry was split up and sent to the museums, it was recorded and logged as to what pieces went where. We are hoping that the two pieces we found will tell us where they had been displayed. The other question is whether or not the museum that had them will know they are missing," I said.

"You mean there's a possibility that the museums don't even know that they've been robbed?" Tom asked, the tone of his voice showing that he couldn't see how a museum wouldn't know that something was missing, especially something so valuable.

"It's possible," I replied.

"How can that be?"

"Tom, some of the museums don't display everything at one time. Sometimes they just don't have room to display everything. Some of it they keep in storage. If they don't check it regularly, they would never know that it is missing," Monica explained.

"Once we find out where this jewelry came from, we can ask them to check and see if any of the rest of what they have is missing. Then we will be able to determine how much was stolen and where it was stolen from," I explained.

"That makes sense, I guess" Tom admitted.

"What do we do now?" Pamela asked.

"We go have brunch. After that we can go ashore to see the sights on the island," I said in a matter of fact tone.

"But if we can go ashore, won't the killer be able to go ashore, too?" Pamela asked.

"Yes, but you have to remember that we are docking at an island. If anyone fails to come back to the ship, we will know who it is and where he is," I explained.

"Anyone not returning to the ship by sailing time will automatically become the primary suspect. We have all the other ways off the island covered by the Coast Guard," I added.

"Oh," Pamela said with a smile.

"I say we go to brunch and then go ashore," Monica suggested as she stood up.

* * * *

The four of us went to the restaurant for brunch. I noticed that Tom and Pamela seemed to be watching the other passengers much more closely than they had yesterday. I guessed that they were looking at them and wondering which one of them might be the killer. There was no way to tell, of course, but I found it interesting to watch Tom and Pamela as they looked at the other passengers with hint of suspicion.

Suddenly, I noticed that Tom seemed more than a little interested in one of the passengers. I turned and looked to see who he was watching. It turned out to be the old man that he had talked to yesterday in the restaurant, Mr. Oliver Higgins.

I took a minute to watch the old man, too. The one thing that seemed to not fit was that he moved like a much younger man than he appeared to be. I had noticed that yesterday, but didn't think much of it at the time. Since I knew his name, I decided that I would ask the Captain to see what he could find out about him. It crossed my mind that maybe I was looking at the passengers with a little more suspicion then I had before the murder.

* * * *

After brunch, the four of us went ashore. I flagged down a carriage for a ride to the main street in Mackinac Island's business district. It was a nice morning with the sun shining and the sky clear. There was a gentle breeze coming in from the southwest.

Once we got to the main street, we decided to walk around a little and visit a few of the local shops. We all bought a little of the famous Mackinac Island fudge and salt water taffy before we got to the end of the street.

We also enjoyed visiting the gift shops and bookstores along the way. I even bought a book about the early sailing ships on the Great Lakes. Once we were finished visiting the town area, we waved down another carriage for a ride up to the Grand Hotel, one of the finest hotels in the country.

On our way to the hotel, we passed the dock near where our ship was moored. I glanced over toward the dock and saw the old man. At first I thought that he looked as if he was lost, but then I got the idea that it might be more than that. It was almost as if he was looking for someone or something.

I watched him for a minute. He first looked one way then the other. He didn't seem to be looking for a carriage to take him some place. I got the impression that he couldn't make up his mind where he wanted to go. He reminded me of someone who felt as if he was trapped, like an animal in a cage unable to escape.

As the carriage moved away from the dock area, I turned and glanced back over my shoulder. The old man just stood there as if he was trying to make up his mind as to what he was supposed to do next. Then he suddenly turned around and went back on board the ship. That was when I lost sight of him.

When I turned back around, I found Monica watching me. I smiled, but I got the feeling that she had seen the old man, too. If she had, there was no doubt in my mind that she knew what I was thinking. The only thing was I didn't want to say anything in front of Tom and Pamela. There was no sense ruining their day. The fact that there had been a murder aboard the ship had made them nervous enough. Monica and I would talk about what we had seen later.

After a visit to the Grand Hotel, we stopped at nearby Fort Mackinaw. The fort had been under several different flags over the years. It had been under French, English and American rule at one time or another in its long history.

It was well after noon before we returned to a little café on Main Street for a late afternoon lunch. Since it was such a pleasant day, we sat out in front under a large Oak tree to eat. I watched the people as they went from one place to another. I even recognized several of the people from the ship. They were making their rounds of the local shops as if nothing had happened. That seemed logical enough since most of the passengers didn't know what had happened aboard the ship.

* * * *

It was while we were enjoying our late lunch that I noticed First Officer Dunbar walking up the street. It looked as if he was headed for an antique shop a few doors down from where we were sitting. He had a small brown paper bag tightly clutched in his hand as if it contained something very important.

The brown paper bag was small, not much bigger than a sandwich bag or a shaving kit. I had to wonder what was in the bag and what he was going to do with it. He turned and went into the antique shop. I had to wonder what reason he had for going into that particular shop.

Monica leaned over to me and whispered in my ear, "What's he up to?"

"I don't know," I replied softly without taking my eyes off him.

"Do you think he is going to try to get rid of some of the jewelry in that antique shop?" she asked.

I know that great minds run on the same track, but this was unreal. I had been wondering the same thing. It wasn't a very smart idea to try to get rid of stolen jewelry here with the Coast Guard all over the place watching every move that everyone from the ship makes. But thieves are not always the smartest people in the world. They often do stupid things. That's why they get caught.

However, First Officer Dunbar would have to have known about the Coast Guard being on the island. After all, he had been sitting in the same room when we discussed it with the Coast Guard Commander earlier this morning.

"What are you two talking about?" Pamela said. "Are you trying to figure out a way to get away from us for awhile?"

"Sort of," I replied with a smile.

"We saw something in that little antique shop earlier. We thought we would like to go back and take another look at it," Monica explained.

"I was thinking that we might take a ride around the island in one of those carriages," Tom said as he turned and looked at Pamela.

"Why don't you and Pamela go ahead? We'll hang around here for a little while. We'll meet you back on the ship for a late dinner," I suggested.

"That sounds good to me. You sure you don't mind if we run off by ourselves?" Tom asked.

"No, not at all," Monica said with a smile.

Pamela and Tom said their good-byes and started off toward an empty carriage that was in front of the café. We watched them as they got in. They told the driver where they wanted to go and they were off.

Monica and I ordered a second cup of coffee. We sipped on the coffee as we waited for First Officer Dunbar to come out of the antique shop.

CHAPTER EIGHT

Monica and I sat at the table in front of the little sidewalk café sipping our coffee and waiting for First Officer Dunbar to come out of the antique shop. I had almost finished my coffee when Monica reached over and lightly touched my arm. I glanced at her and saw that she was looking toward the front of the antique shop. I turned and looked toward the shop just as Dunbar was coming out.

Dunbar stopped for a moment on the porch and looked around. It appeared to me that he was checking to make sure that no one had seen him. I quickly turned back around in the hope that he didn't see me looking at him. I hoped that if he did see me, he might think that I hadn't seen him.

I watched Monica's face to see where she was looking. I could follow his general movements by watching her eyes. As he passed by, I could now watch him without turning around. I noticed that he no longer had the brown paper bag. He had left it in the shop.

I continued to watch Dunbar until he was out of sight. It appeared that he was headed back to the ship with no indication that he was going anywhere else. If that was the case, what was his reason for going to the antique shop?

I quickly let my mind run through all the reasons I could think of for him to pay a visit to that particular shop. I had not seen anything to indicate that the shop did any kind of repairs on antiques so I doubted that he had taken something there for repairs. I didn't see any signs to indicate that the antique shop was a place to sell anything but antiques, which made it the perfect place to take antique jewelry.

There was always the possibility that since Dunbar had made this same trip many times he might have become friends with the shopkeeper. It could be that he was simply delivering something to the shopkeeper that he picked up at one of the other ports of call. That was certainly an explanation, but it didn't set very well with me. There had to be a better explanation.

The package that he dropped off at the antique shop was small enough to have contained a good number of pieces of jewelry, ten or so at least, especially if they were as small as the pieces that I had found. With my suspicious mind working overtime, it made me wonder if maybe the shopkeeper was a fence for stolen jewelry. It could be a place where Dunbar could get rid of some of the loot quickly.

"He doesn't have the bag any more," Monica commented.

"I noticed."

"You think that the bag might have had some of the stolen jewelry in it?"

"It could have, but it seems a little too obvious to me," I replied as I thought about what she had said.

"Maybe, but things are least noticed when they are done out in the open where everyone can see," she reminded me.

"That's true enough. But do you think that he is that smart?"

"I don't know," Monica replied.

I couldn't see Dunbar as that clever. He didn't strike me as the type who could do something criminal right out in the open where anyone who bothered to look could see. He seemed to be much too nervous an individual for that.

"What do we do now?" Monica asked interrupting my thoughts.

"I think it would be a good idea if we went back into that antique shop. We might be able to find out something," I suggested.

"Okay," Monica agreed.

I stood up and motioned for the waiter to come over to our table. After I paid him, Monica and I walked toward the antique shop.

"When we get inside, I want you to go over to the glass display case and take a look at the antique jewelry inside. See if you can identify any of the pieces."

"That's not going to be easy. I'll have to examine them more closely than I can if they're in the display case."

"If you see something that you think is one of the stolen pieces, ask to see it more closely. Whatever you do, don't let on that you're anything more than a tourist that is interested in possibly buying a piece of his jewelry."

Monica nodded her head that she understood.

"And remember, I'll be right there with you," I assured her.

We walked into the shop and immediately began looking around. I walked off to one side to look at a couple of pieces of antique furniture while Monica stopped and looked at some old glass vases and table settings that were near the glass display case.

Monica worked her way to the glass display case that contained quite a bit of antique jewelry, or what looked like it might be antique jewelry. I watched her out of the corner of my eye from a little ways away. I was close enough to hear what she had to say to the owner of the shop, but far enough away to look as if I was more interested in some of the other antiques.

"Is there something that I can help you with?" the shop owner asked with a smile.

"No, I'm just looking at the moment," Monica replied.

"If you see anything that you would like to look at outside the display case, please feel free to ask," he said, and then paused for a moment before turning his attention to me.

I could see him coming toward me. If I could keep him busy for a few minutes, it might give Monica a chance to examine the jewelry a little closer without him realizing what she was doing.

"Is there anything that I can help you with, sir?"

"Well, I'm kind of interested in this old mantel clock."

"That's a very fine piece," he replied with pride.

"What can you tell me about it?" I asked.

"Well, sir, that clock dates back to about seventeen-thirty and was brought over from England around seventeen-eight-three or four. As you can see it is in very good condition."

"Does it work?" I asked as I glanced over his shoulder to see how Monica was doing.

"Most certainly. As a matter of fact it keeps very good time. We don't wind it as it is quite old and we prefer to have the person who purchases it enjoy it however he wishes," he said with a phony sort of smile.

Sure you do, I thought. You want to make sure that whoever breaks it has already bought it, I said silently to myself.

"I might be interested in it if it is not too expensive and if I had a way to get it home safely," I said as I again glanced over his shoulder at Monica.

I could see that Monica was deeply engrossed in what she was doing. She was looking at the jewelry through the glass top of the display case. I wasn't sure if she found something of interest or not, but she seemed to be staring at something in the case.

"That's no problem, I assure you. We ship anything, anywhere. We also insure each and every piece we ship against damage or loss," he said with the kind of smile that sort of sends the message that says, "I've got yah".

I quickly picked up on the fact that he had deliberately avoided telling me what it was going to cost me for the clock. I guessed that it was one of those places where if you have to ask how much it cost, you can't afford it. I didn't press him for the cost of the clock, as I wasn't really interested in it anyway. I was just wasting his time while Monica checked out the jewelry case.

"Let me think about it," I said as I looked at the clock thoughtfully.

"Certainly," he replied with a smile that was as phony as a three-dollar bill.

I watched him as he turned and looked over toward Monica. She was leaning over the glass display case and seemed to be deeply absorbed in one of the pieces of antique jewelry. I could see by the look on the shopkeeper's face that he was thinking that if he couldn't get me to buy something, maybe he could get her interested in something in the glass display case.

As he walked toward Monica, I casually followed him. I wanted to hear everything that was said. I also wanted to be close enough to Monica to get her out of there if things went sour.

Since we had no knowledge of the shopkeeper, we had no idea what would happen if he were involved with the theft of the jewelry. If he was a fence for them, things could get nasty in a hurry if he felt threatened. The last thing I wanted was for Monica to get hurt.

"Do you see something that you would like to examine more closely," he asked very politely as he walked around to the back of the glass display case.

I could see by Monica's reaction that he had startled her. She must have been very engrossed in looking at a piece of jewelry, which gave me a clue that she might have found a piece that should not have been there.

"Oh, ah, yes," she replied politely.

"What is it you would like to see?"

"Two pieces actually. I would like to see this one here in front, the one with the crown on it. And this one over here, the one with the crest," she said as she pointed them out.

"I see that you have very good taste. Those are two of my finest pieces," he said with the grin of a shopkeeper who was sure that he was about to sell something at a great profit.

I watched the owner unlock the doors on the back of the glass display case. He picked out the pieces that Monica had said she wanted to see.

"Here you are," he said as he placed the two pieces of jewelry on a square piece of black velvet.

"I think that you will find no finer examples of Italian craftsmanship than in these two brooches," he said.

Monica picked up the brooch with the crown on it. She held it close as she examined the front of it. She then turned the piece over and looked at the back with the same interest and intensity that she had given the front. The way she was looking at it got me to worrying just a bit.

If this shopkeeper knew anything at all, it would be clear to him that she knew what she was doing. Just from the way she was examining the brooch, he would know that she was not your average tourist. He would know that she knew her stuff, and probably knew it well.

"I see that you have a serious interest in jewelry," he said, the smile on his face seemed forced.

"Oh, I'm really just an amateur," she said with a rather disarming smile.

"I see," he replied.

I got the impression that he saw, all right. She was probably the first customer that he had had in some time that knew what she was looking at. The phony smile disappeared from his face as soon as she looked back at the jewelry.

"This is a very nice brooch," she said as she looked up at him and smiled.

I watched as Monica put the one piece of jewelry back on the square of black cloth and picked up the other. She examined it with the same care and interest as she had given the first piece.

I turned my attention to the shopkeeper. He didn't seem to be so interested in what she was doing as he had. The expression on his face had softened a bit. I had to wonder what she had said that would make him relax and not look so uptight. It had to be her smile and her great looks. Those gorgeous blue eyes of hers could disarm anyone.

"I'm not sure," Monica said with a sigh. "I just don't know which piece I would rather have. They are both very nice.

"What do you think, Honey?" Monica asked as she turned to me.

"Whatever you want, dear," I said as I walked up next to her.

"How much for this one?" Monica asked as she picked up the one with the crown on it.

"That one is just three hundred dollars," he replied. "That's a very good price for that piece.

"I'm sure it is. And the other one?"

"That one is three hundred and fifty dollars," he replied. A bit more expensive, but well worth it as you can see."

"Yes, I see. I don't know. What do you think, Honey?" Monica asked as she set the brooch back on the black cloth.

"I think you might want to think about it for a while. We still have several hours before the ship sails," I suggested.

I could tell by the look on the shopkeeper's face that he wished that I had stayed out of their discussion. Whenever someone says they want to think about it, I'm sure that meant to him that it's a no-sale. The customer is going to leave to "think about it" and never return.

"Okay," Monica replied.

"We'll be back later," I said with a smile.

"Thank you for coming in," the shopkeeper replied as he picked the jewelry up off the black velvet and put it back in the glass display case.

I took Monica by the arm and led her out of the shop. We didn't stop until we were well on our way down the street toward the dock.

* * * *

When we were clear of anyone that might overhear us, I led Monica to a bench under a large oak tree. As soon as we were seated, I turned to her.

"Well, what did you think of the jewelry?" I asked.

"First of all the brooch with the crown on the front was an imitation, but a very good imitation," she said.

"A fake?"

"Yes, but a very good one. It would be worth, maybe, fifty to seventy-five dollars in a top of the line Chicago jewelry store."

"What about the other one?"

"Oh, that one's different. It was real. As real as they come, but it was not as old as it appeared."

"What do you mean?"

"It was the real thing. It was made in Italy and by one of the best twentieth century jewelry makers in Italy at the time. It was probably made somewhere between nineteen-ten to nineteen-twenty. It is worth about one hundred and fifty dollars tops. It's certainly not worth three hundred and fifty dollars he wanted for it."

"So none of them were pieces that we've been looking for?"

"No. I didn't see anything that looked old enough to be from the same period as the ones we saw at the lodge," she said, the tone of her voice showing that she was disappointed.

"I had a thought," I said as I looked at her.

"What's on your mind?" Monica asked.

"There may be a reason that none of those in the shop are from the same period that we're looking for," I said as I thought about the paper bag that Dunbar had left in the shop.

"And why is that?"

"If the shopkeeper is a fence for stolen jewelry, it would be my guess that he didn't have time to get the jewelry out on display before we went into the shop. Then there's always the possibility that he wouldn't put it on display for sale until things cooled down a little, or at least until after the ship sailed."

"That certainly makes a lot of sense, but there's another possibility. Maybe he wasn't supposed to sell the jewelry," Monica suggested.

I looked at her and wondered what was on her mind. Then it hit me. The shopkeeper had given me the answer while he was talking to me. This guy ships things all over the world from that shop. No one would think twice about a package being shipped out of the antique shop to almost anywhere.

"If, and I say, 'IF' this guy is not a fence for the jewelry, he might be a way for them to get the jewelry from one place to another without having to keep it on them. He could ship packages all over the world and no one would be the wiser. You are one smart lady."

"Thank you. If you're right about him being the one to send the stolen jewelry on to some place else, how do we go about finding out? And how do we find out what was in the paper bag?" Monica asked.

This woman could always come up with questions that would make me think. How could we find out if this shopkeeper was a go-between for the thieves? My first thought was to ask Commander Stivers to help us; but without some sort of proof, it would be hard for him to get the State Police involved. Even if he could, it would be difficult for the State Police to get a search warrant for the antique shop without proof. Without that, it would be impossible for us to use any evidence or information we obtained in a court of law.

"We have to find out what was in that paper bag that Dunbar dropped off with the shopkeeper," I said as I tried to think of how we might find that out.

"We could ask First Officer Dunbar what was in the bag," Monica said rather softly, almost as if she was afraid to suggest such a simple way of finding out.

I turned and looked at her. The expression on my face must have told her that I thought she had to be crazy, but I had quickly realized that her idea had merit.

"I guess that isn't a very good idea," she said almost apologetically.

"No. On the contrary, it's not all that bad an idea. Remember what I told you about how Dunbar looked when I arrived at the murder scene?"

"Sure. You said he was green around the gills and that he looked as if he was sick."

"I also told you that I didn't think he was that good an actor when you asked me if I thought he was faking it."

"Yes, I remember."

"I wonder how well he would stand up under some rather pointed questioning." I said, more to help me think about it than to ask Monica a question.

"Do you think he would break?"

"I think the steward would be a lot harder nut to crack than Dunbar. I get the impression that this might be the first time that Dunbar has strayed away from the straight and narrow. If it is, he might buckle under with a little pressure."

"What would happen if he doesn't buckle under?" Monica asked.

"We would be no worse off than we are right now. If we can't get Dunbar to cooperate with us, there's little chance that we could get a search warrant. That would leave us right were we are now.

"How do you plan to handle it?"

"I think I will get him in a room with the Captain and ask him flat out what was in the paper bag he delivered to the shopkeeper."

"Do you think that will do it?" she asked sounding very skeptical.

"I don't know, but at this point it is probably the only thing we can do if we want to know what was in that bag. I doubt that beating around the bush will do it."

"I think we should try to get it done before the ship leaves, don't you?" Monica asked.

"Yes. We have to," I replied.

I stood up and reached out to Monica. She took my hand and we started back to the ship. We wasted no time in getting back on board.

CHAPTER NINE

It was mid-afternoon when we arrived back on the ship. We were unable to talk to the Captain immediately because he was on the bridge attending to his business. We sent a message to him through the Purser stating that we were hoping that we could meet with him before the ship set sail for Marquette, Michigan.

We were relieved when Captain Klausen sent back a message that he would meet with us in the Officers' Mess as soon as he could get there. Monica and I immediately went to the Officers' Mess to wait for him. When we arrived we found the Officers' Mess to be empty. There was no one there.

"Do you think he will let us question Dunbar?" Monica asked.

"I don't know, but I sure hope so. I would think that Captain Klausen, and the cruise line, would want to make sure that none of the officers are involved in anything as serious as murder. If word got out that one of them had killed a passenger, it would not do the cruise line's business any good."

"What if Dunbar wants a lawyer?"

"If he wants a lawyer, the only thing we could do would be to turn him over to the Coast Guard for questioning. I'm sure that he has pretty much the same rights on board this ship as he would on land, but I'm not a hundred percent sure how it works. That might not be the case since the Captain is the ruling authority on the ship as far as I know. I'm not very well informed on the law of the sea. I'm not sure that the law of the sea applies to the Great Lakes, either."

It took about fifteen minutes before Captain Klausen arrived in the Officers' Mess.

"Good afternoon," Captain Klausen said as he entered the room. "I understand that you have something very important to discuss with me."

"Yes, sir," I said. "It has to do with one of your men, First Officer Dunbar to be exact."

"What about Mr. Dunbar?"

I very carefully explained about Dunbar's visit to the antique shop, and the fact that he left whatever was in the brown paper bag at the shop. Captain Klausen sat across the table from us and listened very intently. It was clear to me from the expression on his face that he could see our point of view, but I was left wondering if he was going to let us question Mr. Dunbar.

"Let me see if I understand what it is you want. You want me to allow you to question Mr. Dunbar about what he had in the paper bag that he left at the antique shop."

"That is correct."

"What makes you think that he had anything in the bag that might be related to the investigation of the murder?"

"I'll be perfectly honest with you, sir. The only thing I have going for me is my gut feeling," I replied, probably looking just a little sheepish because I had absolutely no evidence that pointed to Dunbar as having anything to do with the murder.

"And just how good has your "gut feeling" been for you, Mr. McCord?"

"Pretty good most of the time," I replied.

Monica and I sat and watched the Captain as he thought about what I had told him and what I was asking of him. I still wasn't sure from the expression on his face if he was going to allow us to question Dunbar or not.

"Mr. Dunbar is an officer on this ship. A high-ranking officer, I might add. I do not take the idea of allowing you to question him lightly, especially since you don't have anything to go on except your 'gut feeling'."

"I don't take it lightly, either."

"I'm sure you don't. Under normal circumstance I would not allow it without some kind of evidence to suggest that he had done something wrong. However, our circumstances are far from normal. My last communiqué with my superiors instructed me to give you as much latitude as I could in an effort to resolve this unfortunate incident as quickly and quietly as possible. That being the case, I will allow you to question Mr. Dunbar. However, I will allow it only under certain conditions," he added with a tone of authority.

"And what are those conditions, sir?" I asked.

"You will question him here, and in my presence. What is said in this room will stay in this room unless, of course, he confesses to being a part of something that is criminal in nature. Is that agreeable?"

"Yes, sir. At this point, I'm mostly interested in what was in the bag. If it has nothing to do with this case, and I can verify it, I see no reason to pursue Mr. Dunbar any further at this point. I'm looking for a murderer and those who stole the jewelry, that's all. I don't care about anything else.

"However," I added, "if I do discover something of a criminal nature, I will turn what I find over to the United States Coast Guard. Is that agreeable, sir?"

I watched Captain Klausen's eyes for some kind of a reaction. He was very good at keeping what he was thinking to himself. I hoped that he could see things from my perspective.

"Fair enough, Mr. McCord. I'll send for Mr. Dunbar immediately," Captain Klausen said, then stood up and went to the phone on the wall.

I could only hear bits and pieces of what Captain Klausen was saying. However, it was enough for me to know that he was giving someone orders to find Dunbar and have him report directly to the Officers' Mess. Now it was time to sit back and wait for Dunbar to show up.

I looked over at Monica while we waited. She looked back at me and smiled. We were well aware of the fact that we had no authority aboard the ship beyond that which Captain Klausen was willing to give us. We had, however, accomplished our initial objective of getting the chance to question Dunbar. What would come out of it was yet to be seen.

* * * *

While we were waiting for Dunbar, someone knocked on the door. Captain Klausen excused himself and went to the door. When he opened it, I could see that there was a man in ship's uniform standing in the passageway. He handed Captain Klausen a folded piece of paper, then waited for the Captain to respond.

Captain Klausen unfolded the paper and read it. He didn't say anything for a minute or so.

"That will be all," Captain Klausen said, then turned back around.

"Well, it looks like we have some information that will interest you, Mr. McCord," he said as he looked at me.

"What is it?"

"It seems that the Museum of Natural History in Chicago is missing some ninety-four pieces of jewelry from the Samuelson Collection. If my memory serves me correctly, wasn't that the name of the captain who pirated the jewelry off ships on the Great Lakes some hundred years ago?"

"Yes. You are correct. His name was Bartholomew Samuelson and he was a ship's captain on the Great Lakes a hundred years ago. The collection they are referring to is from the stash that Captain Samuelson had at his summer house near Gill's Rock, Wisconsin," Monica said.

"Well, it seems that you were right about that, Doctor Barnhart. It appears that what was stolen has been brought aboard this ship."

"We were pretty sure of that already. We just needed to know how much was stolen and from where so we could identify the pieces if we found them," I said.

"It also appears that Steward James has a criminal record in British Columbia," the Captain added.

"I had a feeling he had a record somewhere. Mostly petty stuff, right?"

"Yes. I believe you would consider it petty. I, on the other hand, do not consider it petty. I have no choice but to dismiss him at the first Canadian port we arrive at. In the meantime, I will have to confine him to his quarters."

"Captain Klausen, I know that I have asked a lot of you. I would like to impose on you one more time."

"What would you like, Mr. McCord?" he asked looking at me with a suspicious look.

"I would appreciate it if you would do me a very big favor. I really would appreciate it if you wouldn't say anything to anyone about Steward James having a criminal record for the time being. If he is involved in something aboard this ship, and I'm sure that he is, I would like to find out what it is before he finds out that we know about his past."

"But you said you didn't think he killed that man," Captain Klausen reminded me, looking somewhat confused by my request.

"I don't think he did, but he's still involved in some way. I just don't know how. I need time to find out to what extent he is involved."

"All right, but when we get to Thunder Bay, I hope you have something by then. If you do not, I will have no choice but to turn him over to the Canadian authorities."

"I understand, and thank you, sir. I appreciate it."

"Let's get back to Mr. Dunbar. From your description of the brown paper bag that Mr. Dunbar had, it would seem to me that it would hardly be big enough to hold very much jewelry, certainly not ninety-four pieces of it."

"You are probably right about that, but you need to remember that it is unlikely that he would have had all the jewelry. Since I don't believe that either Mr. Dunbar or Steward James killed the victim, it would be reasonable to assume that there is at least one other person involved. There may be more.

"If Mr. Dunbar did have any of the jewelry, I would doubt that he had very much. With three people, Steward James, Mr. Dunbar and at least one other splitting up the jewelry, none of them would have very much. I doubt that Mr. Dunbar had even a third of what was stolen as he has been aboard this ship for the past several months."

"Yes, I see your point," Captain Klausen agreed. "What interests me is how he got any of the jewelry at all."

"We are still not sure that he had or has any of it," I reminded the Captain.

"Yes, of course. That is what we hope to find out. Right?"

Just as I was about to answer his question, there was a knock on the Officers' Mess door. Captain Klausen got up and opened the door. I could see Dunbar standing in the hall.

"You wanted to see me, sir?" he asked, his voice upbeat and clear.

"Yes. Come in," Captain Klausen said as he stepped aside so that Dunbar could enter the room.

I watched Dunbar as he walked into the Officers' Mess. The look on his face was that of someone who was concerned about what the Captain wanted to see him about, but not particularly worried about it. However, his expression quickly changed when he noticed Monica and me sitting at the table. He suddenly turned pale and looked a little frightened.

The sudden change of expression led me to believe that he knew more about this murder than he had been willing to admit, or at the least he was involved in something that wasn't on the up and up. I wasn't sure which, but I hoped to find out.

The sudden change in his expression didn't go unnoticed by Monica, either. I felt her hand gently squeeze my leg under the table as she looked up at him.

Dunbar turned and looked at the Captain. He looked like he wanted to say something, but wasn't sure what to say to get the Captain to let him leave. It may not have been clear to the Captain, but it was clear to me that he didn't want to talk to us.

"Have a seat, Mr. Dunbar," I said as I looked up at him.

He didn't immediately sit down. Instead, he looked from me to his Captain and then back to me.

"Sit down, Mr. Dunbar," Captain Klausen instructed him, the tone of his voice showing his authority.

Captain Klausen waited for Dunbar to sit down. Dunbar slowly pulled out a chair and sat down across the table from me. Once he was seated, Captain Klausen pulled up a chair and sat down across the table from Monica.

"Mr. McCord would like to ask you a few questions," Captain Klausen began. "I want you to understand that you are under no obligation to answer any questions that you do not wish to answer. However, I will point out that it is in your own best interest to cooperate fully with Mr. McCord."

"Yes, sir," Dunbar replied with a tone of reluctance in his voice.

"Proceed, Mr. McCord."

"Thank you, Captain," I said, then turned my attention to Dunbar.

"Mr. Dunbar, you said last night that you went to the head about fifteen or twenty minutes before you got the call from Deck Three about the noise. How long were you gone from the bridge?"

"I don't know, ah, maybe, ah fifteen minutes, I guess," he replied a little confused by why I would ask such a trivial question, especially one that I had already asked him.

I could see by the expression on the Captain's face that he was as confused by my question as Dunbar was, but that was the point.

"You went into town early this afternoon, didn't you?"

"Yes. Is that a crime, Mr. McCord?" Dunbar asked, the tone of his voice indicating that he didn't care much for my wasting his time with a bunch of stupid questions.

"No, of course not," I replied with a smile. "I am, however, interested in what you did. What did you do?"

"I went in and did a little shopping as a matter of fact," he replied, as he glanced over at Captain Klausen before looking back at me.

"Where did you shop?"

"I went to several shops."

"Did you buy anything?"

"Actually, no. I didn't see anything that I wanted."

He seemed to be getting a little more relaxed and more comfortable. It was probably because up to now the questions I was asking were non-threatening to him, but that was my objective. I wanted him off balance so that when I asked him something important, I would be able to tell by his expression if he was telling me the truth.

"Did you take anything into town with you?"

Suddenly his eyes got big and he turned a little pale. My question had come as a surprise to him, and he wasn't very good at hiding his surprise. He must have realized that we had seen him with the paper bag.

"I don't understand," he said as he quickly glanced over at the Captain.

The Captain was simply leaning back in his chair and watching what was going on. I was positive that Captain Klausen noticed the sudden change of expression on Dunbar's face, too.

"It's a simple enough question, Mr. Dunbar. Did you or did you not take anything into town with you?" I asked, the tone of my voice insisting on an answer.

Dunbar looked over at the Captain almost as if he was pleading for the Captain to get him out of there. I got the impression that he was trying to figure out just how much I knew and how much the Captain knew. He seemed to be more afraid of the Captain than of my questions which interested me.

"Answer the question, Mr. Dunbar," Captain Klausen ordered.

"No, ah, yes," he stuttered.

"Which is it, yes or no?" I asked.

"Ah, yes," he said softly after a long sigh.

"What did you take into town?"

"A paper bag."

The expression on his face gave me the impression that he was almost begging me not to make him tell what was in the bag, at least in front of his Captain. I was not about to give him that option.

"What was in the bag, Mr. Dunbar?"

Dunbar glanced over at the Captain, and then looked back at me. It was as plain as day that he had something to hide. The only question that needed to be answered was what was he hiding?

"I think it would be in your best interest to answer Mr. McCord's question. You're already in enough trouble with me," Captain Klausen said, the tone of his voice showing that he had little patience left with Dunbar's reluctance.

Dunbar dropped his head down and looked at his hands that were folded in front of him on the table. Slowly he looked up at me, took in a deep breath, and then let out a long sigh.

"I was doing a favor for James, Billy James, the steward."

"What was the favor?"

Looking around, it was clear to him that there was nothing else he could do but to tell us everything. It was over for him and he knew it.

"I took the bag to the antique shop for James."

"What was in the bag?"

"Don't know. I was just delivering the bag to the shop-keeper at that antique shop."

"You mean you never looked in the bag?"

"No, sir."

"You never looked in the bag, but I'd be willing to bet that you had a pretty good idea what was in the bag."

Dunbar did not respond. The look on his face gave me my answer.

"You may not have known what was in the bag, but I suspect that you knew that the bag contained things that James had stolen from passengers aboard this ship. Am I right?"

"Yes, sir," he admitted reluctantly.

"Then why did you do it if you knew the bag contained stolen property?"

"I owed him."

"You owed him? Do you mind explaining that?"

Dunbar looked at the Captain before he started to explain.

"I got into a poker game with James and two other hands aboard the ship while we were in port a few days ago. I lost quite a bit of money and didn't have the money to cover my bets. James loaned me the money to cover them and told me that I could pay him back later."

"What did you take that to mean?" I asked.

"I thought that he would let me pay him back on payday. But when payday came, he told me there was no hurry."

"Do you think he knew about Wright and Lancaster and the stolen jewelry and was planning on stealing a little for himself?"

"No, I don't think so. He would have no way of knowing what jewelry would be on board."

"What makes you think that he wouldn't know?"

"We don't see the passenger list until we dock. We have no advanced information on any of the passengers."

I looked over at the Captain. He nodded his head to indicate that what Dunbar had said was true.

"I'm done with you for now, but I don't want a word of what you said here to leak out. If you have dealings with James, you simply tell him that you delivered the bag to the shopkeeper and left. You understand?" I asked.

"Yes, sir."

"Mr. Dunbar, you will return to your duties without a word of this conversation to anyone. How you conduct yourself for the rest of this trip will help determine the discipline that you will receive when we get back to our homeport. Do you understand?" Captain Klausen said, the tone of his voice showing that he was not at all happy with Dunbar.

"Yes, sir," he replied, his voice showing that there was still some hope that he wouldn't lose his position as First Officer.

We waited for Dunbar to leave the room. After he left we asked Captain Klausen to notify the United States Coast Guard and have the stolen jewelry recovered from the shopkeeper and place him under arrest for accepting stolen merchandise. The Captain assured us that he would do that and left the Officers' Mess.

Monica and I returned to our suite to relax and to wait for more information on the dead man. I also wanted to see a copy of the criminal report on Steward James. I needed to know how well James was connected with other criminals, and how serious his criminal background really was. The seriousness of his criminal background could give us some idea of what kind of a criminal he was, but that was still no guarantee that he had not changed his MO and moved up to something far more serious.

CHAPTER TEN

It seemed that Monica and I had no more than returned to our suite and sat down on the loveseat when there was a knock on the door. We hadn't even had a chance to talk over what we had been told by Dunbar. I looked at Monica and she looked at me. It seemed that we were never going to get a chance to spend any time alone together.

I walked over to the door and looked through the peephole. Standing in front of the door was one of the ship's officers. I reluctantly opened the door wondering what had happened now.

"Yes? What is it?" I asked.

"Captain Klausen instructed me to give this to you, sir. He said that you would find it most interesting," the young officer said as he held out a large envelope.

I looked at the envelope for a second before I took it from the ship's officer. I was expecting some information, but I didn't think that it would get here so quickly.

"Thank you," I said as the young officer stepped back.

I closed the door, turned around and looked toward Monica. I could see that she was looking at the envelope.

"What's that?" she asked.

"I don't know for sure, but my guess would be that it's the criminal record on Steward James. The officer that delivered it said it was from the Captain and that I would find it very interesting."

"Open it and let's see."

I opened the envelope as I sat down on the loveseat next to Monica. I started dumping out the contents of the envelope on the coffee table in front of us.

There were two memos, each attached to an inventory list of jewelry, a memo attached to an autopsy report and a copy of the criminal record on one Billy D. James, the steward. I glanced in the envelope to see if anything might have been left inside. I noticed one half-page memo.

"Well, what do we have here," I said as I reached in the envelope and pulled out the memo.

The half-page memo was from Commander Stivers. I read it carefully.

The memo read:

Mr. McCord,
Blood samples and hair fibers found on the victim were those of the victim and one other person. We are unable to identify the other person at this time.
Will keep in touch.
Cmd Stivers, USCG."

"It seems that not all the blood in the cabin belonged to our victim. They found blood and hair samples from two people," I said as I looked at Monica.

"That means there were two people injured in that room."

"It would appear that our victim may have drawn blood from his assailant."

"Here's the autopsy report on the victim," Monica said holding it out to me. "I would prefer that you read it. These things tend to make me a little squeamish."

It was not hard for me to understand her feelings. I had seen a lot of autopsy reports in my career as a policeman and reading them was still a part of the job that I hated doing.

I took the report and began reading it. The first thing I noticed was the name of the victim. It was William F. Lancaster of Calumet City, Illinois, the same name as in the wallet of the man we found dead in the cabin. However, the First Officer had identified the same man as Frank Wright from Chicago, and the cabin he was found in had been registered to Frank Wright.

The first thing that crossed my mind was why would a man give a false name for a pleasure cruise on a ship? He wouldn't. He had to be hiding from someone, or hiding something.

The autopsy report stated that the victim had bruises consistent with a rather violent struggle, a broken neck at the fourth and fifth cervical vertebrae, and two puncture wounds to the chest. The puncture wounds were consistent with the knife that had been sent to the lab as the suspected murder weapon. The knife had blood and tissue that was a match to the victim. The fatal wound was inflicted when the weapon had entered the victim's chest just to the left of the sternum, slipping between the ribs and puncturing the left lower ventricle of the heart. The cause of death was listed as, "Death by stabbing by unknown assailant".

The report indicated that it was believed that either of the two serious injuries would have produced death. However, it was felt that the knife wounds were inflicted before the victim's neck was broken. The report simply reinforced what I believed to have happened.

"Whoever killed William Lancaster was a rather violent person, and he wanted to make sure that Lancaster was dead," I said more to myself than to Monica.

"Do you happen to know who William Lancaster was?" Monica asked.

"No," I replied after giving it some thought. "Do you?"

"No, but I think it would be a good idea if we find out."

"I certainly agree. I'll ask the Captain to contact Commander Stivers and see if he can find out anything about Lancaster. I wouldn't be surprised if he has a prison record somewhere. My guess would be in Illinois or Wisconsin, possibly both."

"Nick, these two inventory lists show that there were eighty-three pieces of jewelry stolen from the Samuelson Collection from the Milwaukee Museum, and ninety-four pieces stolen from the Chicago Museum. That means that two museums were hit, not just one."

"Really?"

"Yes. Both museums have had pieces stolen. In fact, it appears as if the entire jewelry part of the collection from both museums were stolen," Monica said thoughtfully as she looked at the lists.

"Was anything other than jewelry taken from the Samuelson Collection?"

"Not according to the inventory lists. It shows that just the jewelry was taken."

"That being the case, I'd almost be willing to bet that they were hit within hours of each other," I said as I thought about it. "I'd also be willing to bet that the jewelry from both museums is somewhere on this ship."

"The memos attached to the inventory lists don't give us a time frame to work from. We have no idea when the robberies took place," Monica reminded me.

"That might have been helpful to know," I said.

"It appears that no one did a very good job of keeping tabs on the jewelry. They didn't even know that the pieces were missing until we made our inquiry into them," Monica said, her disbelief in the museums' poor inventory control showed on her face.

"Are either of the two pieces we found on the inventory lists?" I asked.

I watched Monica as she carefully went over the lists. I noticed her eyes light up as she turned and looked at me.

"How did you know that the jewelry from both museums would be here?" she asked as she looked at me.

"I didn't, it was just a wild guess."

"Well, you guessed right."

"What do you mean?"

"Of the two pieces you found in the cabin, one is from the Milwaukee Museum, and the other is from the Chicago

Museum. In other words, they're from different robberies," she said with a grin.

Since neither of the museums could pinpoint the time when the jewelry had disappeared, I felt that it was most likely that the museums were hit one right after the other. That type of robbery takes timing, planning and skill. Whoever pulled off the robberies knew what they were doing and how to get it done.

"There's an interesting comment in these memos," Monica said. "Both memos list the name of the security company that handles their alarm systems. They are both handled by A-1 Security Incorporated out of Chicago."

"Are you saying that both of the museums use the same security company to install their security systems?"

"Yes," she said with a grin. "And to maintain them, too."

It was obvious to me that Monica understood the importance of that vital piece of information. If they both had the same security company, then there was a good chance that whoever robbed the two museums knew how the systems worked from the inside. That made it very clear to me what our next move was to be.

"I'll call the Captain and see if he can get me in touch with Commander Stivers. I would like to see who works for A-1 Security Incorporated," I said as I reached over and picked up the phone.

I explained what we wanted and Captain Klausen said that he would contact Commander Stivers right away. He also agreed to ask Commander Stivers to check for any criminal record for Lancaster.

After I hung up the phone, I got to thinking. On board this ship there was at least one other person that was involved with the robbery. The person who had killed Lancaster, for sure, but I had a feeling that there had to be others, at least one other.

Checking the records of the security company was a long shot at best, but it was all we had at the moment. It could provide us with a link to the killer.

As soon as Monica and I had gone over the rest of the reports, we decided that we should go to the restaurant for dinner. It was getting close to the time when the restaurant would be closing for the night.

We put the information back in the envelope and set it aside. We changed and left the suite for the restaurant.

* * * *

As we walked into the restaurant, we found it to be almost empty of people. Monica noticed Tom and Pamela sitting at a table near a window and pointed them out to me. I was a little surprised at myself, as I had not given them a thought for the better part of the day.

It looked as if they were getting ready to order their dinner. Tom looked up and saw us. He smiled and motioned for us to join them.

"Shall we?" Monica asked.

"Sure. I wonder how their day went."

We walked across the room to the table where Tom and Pamela were sitting.

"Where have you two been all day?" Tom said as we sat down.

"In our room for a good part of it," I replied casually.

I noticed the grin that came over Pamela's face as she looked at Monica. Tom had an "I know what you were doing" sort of grin on his face. The funny part of it was that he had absolutely no idea what we had been doing. We had not spent most of our day in our room, but I could see no reason to ruin their day by telling them the truth.

"We had a great time. We took a nice casual ride in a carriage around the island after we left you guys," Tom said.

"Yes. It was very nice," Pamela added as she looked at Tom with a dreamy look in her eyes.

I'm sure Monica didn't miss seeing Pamela reach over and put her hand on top of Tom's. I noticed it. It was becoming clear that they were so wrapped up in each other that they had no idea what was going on around them. The murder on the ship had not seemed to register for them past when they were told about it. They were in a world all their own most of the time, and I have to admit I was feeling a little envious of them.

We ordered our dinner, and then the four of us sat eating and talking about the sights they had seen on the island. Monica and I made it a point of not discussing the investigation with them. I think we were both convinced that it would serve no useful purpose.

Monica and I were listening to Tom and Pamela telling us about a couple that they had seen who were riding a bicycle built for two around the island. They were apparently newlyweds and were being rather playful. They lost their balance and control of the bicycle when they tried to kiss each other while riding. The end result was they accidentally went off the road and ended up in the lake. Fortunately, they were not injured and soon began laughing at themselves when they realized how silly they must have looked.

We were all having a good laugh over the story when one of the ship's officers came across the room toward our table. He had in his hand one of those large envelopes that Captain Klausen used. I instantly knew that the Captain had come up with more information for us.

At that moment, I was feeling like it was another day at the office. It certainly didn't feel like I was on the ship for our honeymoon.

"Mr. McCord, this is from Captain Klausen," the young officer said as he handed me the envelope.

"Thank you," I said and took the envelope from him.

Without another word, the officer turned and left the room. I slipped the envelope down along side my chair and leaned forward on my elbows to listen to more about Tom and Pamela's day. However, no one was talking any more. That simple envelope had suddenly turned everyone very quiet.

Tom and Pamela sat looking at me as if they were not only waiting for me to open the envelope, but expected me to open it now so they could see what the Captain had sent me. From the look on Monica's face, I think Monica was hoping that I wouldn't open it at all.

"Aren't you going to open it?" Tom finally asked, unable to control his curiosity any longer. "It isn't everyone who gets a personal letter from the Captain."

"It can wait. It's just some information that I requested from him."

I got this sudden feeling that Tom and Pamela were starting to remember what had happened. Tom began talking about their day, but the otherwise friendly, enjoyable conversation seemed to take on a more serious tone. Oh, they still talked about the island and what they had seen and done, but there was an underlying seriousness that took the humor and fun out of the conversation.

When things got quiet, I noticed Tom glance at his watch and then look at me. I got the impression that he was looking for an excuse to end the evening without hurting anyone's feelings. I couldn't blame him for that. I was ready to end the evening, too.

"I think we've all had a pretty long day. What do you say that we call it a night," Tom finally suggested.

"I think that's a good idea," Monica replied as she looked at me.

"I am a little tired," Pamela admitted as she looked over at Tom.

We all sort of agreed that it was time to go to our cabins. We all got up and started across the room. Monica and I sort of followed along behind Tom and Pamela.

As we turned down the passageway toward our suite, I saw the old man, Mr. Higgins, coming down the hall toward us. As he passed Tom, Higgins accidentally brushed against Tom in the narrow passageway. I happened to be looking right at Mr. Higgins' face when he did. I couldn't say for sure, but I got the impression from the look on his face that brushing against Tom had caused him some pain. He acted as if he was reaching for his arm, but when he noticed that I was watching him, he quickly straightened his shoulders and moved on down the hall, quickening his pace.

"Excuse me," I heard Mr. Higgins say as he continued down the hall.

The incident confused me a little. It didn't look to me as if he had run into Tom hard enough to have done anything more than lightly brush against him. The more I thought about it, the more I felt that I was overreacting to what I thought I saw. It happened so quickly that I might have misread the look on the old man's face. Mr. Higgins had not been paying attention to where he was going. He was probably just reacting to the surprise of almost running into Tom. I was tired and maybe I didn't really see anything, I thought.

After I unlocked the door to our suite, I glanced down the hall to where the old man had gone. I watched him as he turned and went up the stairway. I then turned and went into our suite.

"What's the matter?" Monica asked me.

"Oh, nothing. I guess I'm just tired."

"I know just what will take care of that," Monica said with a sexy smile.

"What do you have in mind, Doctor Barnhart?"

"A warm shower and a good night's rest are what this doctor orders."

"I think I could handle that," I replied with a grin.

I dropped the envelope next to the chair and walked over to Monica. I slipped my arms around her and pulled her up against me.

After a long, passionate kiss, we began to undress each other. It wasn't long before we were enjoying a nice warm shower together. The feel of her body under my hands and against my chest was all I needed to take away the stress of the day.

After a long shower, we dried each other and climbed into the bed. It was not long before we were wrapped in each other's arms and in each other's love.

After our lovemaking, we curled up together and drifted off into a restful sleep. A sleep that we needed and we didn't want disturbed.

CHAPTER ELEVEN

In the quiet of the early morning hours, I could hear the almost inaudible hum of the ship's engines as I lay in bed. The steady drone of the engines was nothing that anyone would really notice when there were any other noises. I found it to be a rather soothing sound. One that reassured a person that everything was as it should be, but I knew better. Everything was not as it should be.

There was no reason for me to be awake so early in the morning. I had the most beautiful woman in the world lying beside me in a large comfortable bed, and the ship was running smoothly in the quiet blue waters of Lake Superior.

The only reason I could think of for being awake was that my mind was full of unanswered questions. Questions like who was William Lancaster, and why was he dead? Who stole the jewelry from the museums? Was it Lancaster or someone else? Who had been working with Lancaster?

Unable to sleep, I carefully slipped out of bed in the hope of not waking Monica. I picked up the large envelope that I had been given last night and tiptoed into the bathroom. I sat down on the stool and opened the envelope I had received from the Captain last evening.

Inside, I found a note from Captain Klausen. It simply stated that all the passengers who had gotten off the ship at Mackinac Island had returned to the ship and were accounted for.

I wasn't sure how that bit of news made me feel. In a way I would have liked to have had someone missing so that I would have at least one solid suspect, and a name to go along with the title of murderer. On the other hand, it was a relief to know that the murderer was still on the ship. It seemed to be less important for me to know the name of the murderer than it did to know that he had not gotten away, yet.

The second item was the criminal record on one William F. Lancaster. As I looked over his record, I found that he had been arrested several times, but only served a few years in jail. Most of the charges ended up being plea bargained down to almost nothing, or never went to trial for one reason or another. I read that he had been incarcerated at the Illinois Correctional Facility at Joliet for five years of a ten-year sentence which would indicate that he had been a model prisoner.

Further examination of the report showed that he had also been incarcerated in a Wisconsin correctional institution. It was noted that he had recently been released from the Dodge Correctional Institution at Waupun, Wisconsin, a maximum-security prison northwest of Milwaukee. I was familiar with that prison. During my years as a police officer I had arrested a number of criminals who were eventually sent there.

Lancaster's criminal report was rather long and appeared to be very complete. It showed that he had been arrested several times for "smash and grab" armed robbery, mostly of jewelry stores. After reading about all the jewelry stores that he had robbed or been accused of robbing, I couldn't help but think that robbing a museum didn't seem to fit his pattern.

It seemed to me that robbing jewelry stores, especially in the manner that Lancaster used, didn't take a great deal of knowledge of jewelry. To rob a jewelry store like he did, all one had to do was smash the glass case and grab anything that looked expensive. That would mean that he would grab diamonds, gold items and things like that. It would be fairly easy to pick out those things that could be turned into cash quickly by selling them to about any fence in town.

Based on my experience as a police officer and detective, it took a special kind of thief to heist a museum.

They had to know what they were after and how to get rid of it once they got it. You couldn't just sell it on any street corner. That being the case, he would have to have someone to buy what he stole. That meant he would have to steal the right things in order to get his buyer to take them off his hands quickly.

Lancaster's criminal report gave no indication that he knew very much about museum jewelry. Museum jewelry was often far more valuable because it was rare and often quite old. It was more valuable to a collector than the sum value of its gold, silver or the gems it contained. For Lancaster to rob a museum didn't make a whole lot of sense.

The last item in the envelope was a fax from A-1 Security, Inc. It was a list of names of the people who were working for the security company that had installed and/or maintained the security systems in museums and jewelry stores that had been robbed in the past five years. The list was quite long, but it didn't take me long to recognize one of the names on the list. The name was that of Frank Wright.

Under the column labeled "Job Title" for Frank Wright were the words, "Maintenance Technician". That was all I needed to see. A maintenance technician would certainly know everything there was to know about the security system including how it worked and how to get past it. Now I had a pretty good idea of how they got past the museums' security systems.

The next column on the fax listed the date of hire followed by the date of termination. The date of hire showed that Frank Wright had worked for A-1 Security, Inc. for over twenty years. There was nothing in the column for termination. It was a little puzzling that there was no termination date. I had to ask myself if he was still employed by A-1 Security, Inc.

The information from A-1 Security, Inc. sure helped answer one question. Frank Wright had to have been the one to get William Lancaster into the museums without setting off the security alarms, but something was very wrong with the picture that was forming in my mind.

It was clear that Frank Wright and William Lancaster were not one and the same person as was originally thought on the night that Lancaster's body was found. The body had been identified as Frank Wright by several of the ship's crew, and the room was registered to Frank Wright. Yet, Lancaster was the one found dead in the room and the one identified by the steward as Frank Wright.

It suddenly occurred to me that I had not checked the ship's register to see if William Lancaster was also a passenger. If he was, then there was a fair chance that I would find Wright in Lancaster's room. There had not been any mention of a Frank Wright on the ship other than the person now known as Lancaster. That led me to believe that there was no Frank Wright on board.

Since the Coast Guard had the body of William Lancaster, I had to wonder where Frank Wright might be found. The fact that Lancaster had registered aboard the ship as Frank Wright indicated that only one of them had planned on being aboard the ship, and that was Wright.

I leaned back against the toilet tank and closed my eyes. I had to take a moment to think. Everything has an explanation and this was no different. All I had to do was find it. The more I thought about it, the more I had to think that Frank Wright had probably never even been aboard the ship.

Logic told me that if Lancaster was posing as Wright, then it was a good bet that Wright was dead and his body had simply not been found, yet. If that was the case, then who killed Lancaster? If what I believed to be true was true, then there had to be a third party involved. That third person was the one who had killed Lancaster.

It was clear what had to be done. I needed descriptions of both Frank Wright and William Lancaster in order to separate the two. I also needed to know if Frank Wright showed up for work in the last few days. I doubted that he had, but it would clear up a lot to know for sure.

There was one other thing that crossed my mind as I sat thinking. Since the report on Lancaster showed that he had gotten out of jail recently, how did he have time to set up the robbery of both museums? My answer was that he didn't. It had to have been someone else that masterminded the robberies. Was it Wright, or someone else?

I decided that I would like to know who else got out of the same prison at about the same time as Lancaster. It would also be a good idea to find out who might have visited him over the past few months. I didn't feel that with the time frame, from the time Lancaster got out of jail to the time the ship set sail, was long enough to plan such a robbery, especially if the two museums were hit on the same night and were located in two different cities. It had to have taken time to set it up, time that Lancaster could not have had unless it was all planned while he was still in jail.

* * * *

Suddenly there was a light tap on the bathroom door. It quickly brought me out of my thoughts.

"Are you all right, Nick?"

I could hear the concern in Monica's voice. I don't know how long I had been in the bathroom, but it must have been for a considerable length of time.

"Yeah, I'm fine," I said as I stuffed the papers back in the envelope.

By the time I came out of the bathroom, Monica had returned to the bed, but she had not gone back to sleep. I noticed the worried look on her face. There was no doubt in my mind that she was concerned about me. But as soon as she saw that I had the envelope in my hand, she seemed to relax.

"I didn't want to disturb you," I said.

A smile came over her face that said I was forgiven for causing her to worry. I set the envelope down next to the chair and climbed back into bed with her. As soon as I laid down, she curled up against me.

"I hope you haven't solved this case without me," she whispered softly, her voice sounding very sexy.

"No. I'm going to need all the help I can get on this one," I said with a note of frustration.

"What was in the envelope?"

"Do you really want to know?"

"Of course. We are in this together, remember?"

I quickly conceded that she was right. I took the next little while to tell her about everything in the envelope. After that, I told her what I thought and why I had come to the conclusions that I had, then I waited for her to respond.

"I have been thinking about it, too. I think finding out who has gotten out of prison at the same time as Lancaster is a good idea, but I think there may be something that we have overlooked."

"What's that, Honey?"

"Did either of the museums list anything as being stolen that was not part of the Samuelson Collections?"

I had to think about her question for a moment. I couldn't remember seeing anything on the list of stolen items that hadn't been part of the collections, but then I couldn't remember everything on the list, either.

"I don't know for sure. That would be something you would know better than I. You'd have to go over the lists and tell me. What's going on in that pretty little head of yours?" I asked as I gently squeezed her.

Monica rolled up on top of me and stretched her long, slender body over me. After a brief but loving kiss, she rose up and propped her face in her hands as she looked down into my eyes.

"Think of this. You have two separate robberies of museums where we think that the only things taken were pieces of jewelry from a specific collection. Nothing else was apparently touched. What does that tell you?"

"It tells me that you are one sexy lady and I like the feel of your seductive body against me," I replied with a big grin.

"Come on. Get serious," she replied playfully.

"I am serious, but okay. It makes me think that whoever robbed the two museums knew exactly what they were after, and that they were not about to waste time taking anything else."

"That's true, but doesn't it also tell you that they must have had a buyer all lined up for the stolen jewelry?" she asked.

I had thought about it, but at the time had nothing that would indicate that to be the case. I had dismissed it from my mind for the time being, and for some reason I couldn't explain at the moment. I forgot it probably because I had so many things on my mind. It was hard for me to believe that I had forgotten that very strong possibility.

"Now I know why I love you," I said as I let my hand slide down across the small of her back and over her firm smooth butt.

"We need to go over the lists of stolen jewelry very closely to be sure that my theory is a good one," she said.

"Even if there were other pieces of jewelry taken, it's still a good theory. They may have taken a few other items by mistake, or they weren't sure what pieces actually belonged to the collections that they wanted to steal."

"Then there's the possibility that they took other pieces of jewelry in an effort to lead the trail away from their real purpose," Monica said thoughtfully.

"Very true. In either case, there would only be a few items that were not part of the collection."

"You're probably right. What do we do now?" Monica asked.

"Are you asking me what I want to do right now, this very minute?" I said as I squeezed her tightly against me.

"No, not really. I think I know what you would like to do right now," she said with a giggle.

"Any objections?"

"No, none at all," she replied as she slowly leaned down until our lips met.

Monica and I spent the next hour or so kissing and touching. It wasn't long before we were making love to each other. Afterwards, we spent some time in the shower together before getting dressed.

As we dressed, we once again began to talk about some of the things we had to do to get answers to some of our questions. We needed to get hold of A-1 Security, Inc. to find out if Frank Wright was at work. We also needed to get a list of prisoners that had been released from the same prison and at about the same time as Lancaster, and a list of any contacts Lancaster might have had during the last few months he was incarcerated. We also needed to get a detailed list of all the items stolen other than from the collection and go over it to see if Monica's theory would hold up.

It was mid-morning by the time we left our suite. Since it was too early for lunch and too late for breakfast, we decided that we would stop in the lounge for mid-morning brunch. Experience had taught us that the ship's brunch was excellent.

As we entered the lounge, we saw Tom and Pamela sitting alone in a large booth in the corner. Tom was leaning close to Pamela and talking very softly as if he didn't want anyone to hear him. I noticed that they were holding hands. I wasn't sure if we should disturb them, but we walked over to them anyway.

"Hi," I said.

As Pamela looked up at us, I could see that she had been crying. There were still tears on her cheeks and her eyes were red. I had to wonder if Tom was the reason that she was upset.

"What's the matter, Pamela," Monica asked as she sat down next to her and put her arm around Pamela's shoulders.

Pamela squeezed Tom's hand as she smiled at Monica.

"Tom just asked me to marry him this morning," she said as Tom handed her a handkerchief.

"I take it by all the tears that the answer was "yes"? I asked as I looked at Tom.

"Yes," he replied with a silly grin.

"I know this is none of my business, but isn't this a little sudden?" I asked.

"Yes, it is," Tom agreed.

"I know it's kind of sudden, but I really think we love each other," Pamela said as she looked at Monica.

Tom looked like he was happier than I had seen him in a long time. Pamela looked like she could hardly believe that Tom would want her. I couldn't figure out for the life of me why he wouldn't. She was nice, beautiful, and apparently crazy about him.

"Well, I think this calls for a toast," I said as I slid out of the booth.

I went over to the bar and ordered a bottle of champagne and four glasses. As I waited for the bartender to get it, I looked back over at the booth. Tom had always been my best friend. Today was something very special for him. This was the first time since we graduated from college that I had seen him really happy. I thought it was kind of sudden, but then who was I to say. Monica and I fell in love within a day or two of when we first met. Why couldn't Tom and Pamela? The only difference was that we had had more time to get to know each other.

As I headed back to the table with the bottle of Champagne, I noticed that Monica had moved to the other side of the booth and was sitting across from Tom. I slid in beside her and poured a glass of bubbly for each of us. I raised my glass to present a toast.

"To two very special people. May they have a long and enjoyable life together with nothing but dreams that come true."

With that said, we all touched our glasses together then drank down the contents.

We spent the rest of the morning talking about weddings, mostly ours, and about the places that we had all seen. We didn't eat anything so when it came time for lunch, we all were pretty hungry and went to the restaurant together.

CHAPTER TWELVE

Upon entering the restaurant, the headwaiter led us to a table that was located near a window. Pamela was seated with her back to the window with Tom to her left. I was seated across the table from Tom, and Monica was seated directly across the table from Pamela.

Monica and I sat and listened while Tom told Pamela about his lodge on Gill's Point in Wisconsin, and about the old mine that had a secret tunnel leading to it from the house. She seemed fascinated by it and thought it sounded like a wonderful place. Its sordid history seemed to make it more intriguing for her, as it seemed to have for others.

I wasn't sure what Pamela did for a living or where she was originally from, but I did know that she lived in Chicago. It made me wonder how she would like it living miles from any town bigger than a few thousand people.

I looked over at Monica and smiled. She seemed interested in the conversation. I, however, found my attention drawn to the window by a movement that I caught out of the corner of my eye. I could see the side of the face of Mr. Higgins, who had been of such interest to Tom. I couldn't see what he was doing, but he was looking off into the distance. Whatever he was looking at seemed to hold his attention.

"What are you looking at?" Tom asked.

"Oh, nothing special," I replied.

Tom turned and looked out the window, then turned back.

"That's the old man we see in the passageways all the time. It's almost as if he has nothing to do but walk around the ship. You know, I even saw him in the passageway on the other side of the ship when I went to get my briefcase," Tom said.

"Really?" Monica asked.

"Yeah. He came around the corner into the hall just as I was going into the cabin. I only got a glimpse of him, but you know it's funny," Tom said, then looked off toward the window again.

"What's funny, Tom."

Tom turned back and looked at me, then said "What?"

"I asked what was funny about the old man?"

"Oh. He seemed very interested in watching me go into that cabin. For the life of me, I don't know what difference it could possibly make to him. It wasn't even my cabin."

"Maybe that's why he looked at you the way he did," I suggested.

"I don't know, but I don't think so. I still think I know him," Tom said.

I looked out the window again to where the old man had been, but he was gone. I don't know why I had become so interested in the old man, but he kept coming up in my thoughts almost as much as he kept showing up around the ship. Maybe it was because we kept running into him, but that didn't seem to be the reason. After all, we were bound to run into each other quite often as we were all on a fairly small cruise ship.

The more I thought about it, the more I wondered about him. I closed my eyes for a moment or two and tried to picture him in my mind. It was important to me to try to picture every little detail that I could remember about him including the shape of his ears, the look of his eyes, his build, the way he walked and anything else I could observe.

"What's the matter?" Monica asked, with a tone of concern in her voice.

I quickly opened my eyes as I realized that she was talking to me. I felt a little embarrassed as if she had caught me sleeping.

"Nothing," I replied sheepishly.

I wanted to tell her what was going through my mind, but I didn't want to say anything in front of Tom and Pamela. From the look on Monica's face, she got my message and said nothing more about it. I felt that a quick change of subjects was in order.

"What are you going to do while we are in Marquette?" I asked as I looked at Tom.

"I don't know," he said as he turned and looked at Pamela for an answer or a suggestion.

"I would like to take the "Anatomy of A Murder" tour. I would like to see where some of the movie was filmed," Pamela said with a note of excitement in her voice. "What do the two of you want to do?"

"I would like to take a tour of a couple of the lighthouses in the area. "I've always been fascinated by them," Monica said with a smile.

"Oh," Pamela said with a look of disappointment, apparently thinking that Monica's suggestion would win out over hers.

"We don't have to go see the same things," I said with a grin. "I'm sure that you and Tom would like to wonder off by yourselves anyway. We don't need a baby-sitter, and I'm sure you guys don't want one, either," I said with a grin.

"After lunch, we can go our way and they can go theirs," Tom said to Pamela.

"We can meet back here for dinner or for a late evening drink in the lounge if you like," Pamela suggested.

"Sounds good to me," I agreed.

I looked around at the rest, and they all seemed to think that Pamela's suggestion was a good one. Once we had that settled, we ate our lunches and returned to our cabins to get ready for an afternoon of fun in the sun.

Once we were in our suite, Monica looked over at me and asked, "What were you thinking about before our lunch came? I got the impression that you didn't want to say anything in front of Tom and Pamela."

"I was thinking about that old man that we are always seeing around the ship. You know, Mr. Higgins I believe he calls himself."

"What about him? You sound as if you don't think his real name is Higgins."

"I'm not sure what I believe about him."

I went on to explain to her my thoughts about the old man. The fact that he didn't seem to move like the old man he appeared to be, and the fact that he always seemed to be watching Tom made me wonder about him. There was also the fact that there was this gut feeling I had that he wasn't who he said he was, and how that all kept working on my subconscious.

"Well, I think that you should put him out of your mind for a little while so we can enjoy at least some of this trip."

"You're right, Honey. Let's go ashore and take the tour of the lighthouses."

* * * *

As soon as we were ready to leave the ship, we left our suite and walked to the deck where the gangplank was located. I could see several people making their way down the gangplank and disappearing into the various shops, tour places or simply into the town. That thought caused me to think about our killer. He could walk off the ship as easy as any other passenger and disappear into the crowd, never to be seen again.

"Nick, you're not giving me your undivided attention," Monica reminded me.

"You're right," I replied as I took hold of her hand and started down the gangplank.

"What are you thinking about?" she asked.

"I'm wondering if our killer will suddenly disappear now that we are in a place where he could go anywhere without anyone knowing," I replied.

"Are you still so sure that he is on the ship?"

"No, not really. It would be nice to think so, though."

I had noticed that the people leaving the ship were being watched over by the ship's crew. It didn't look like there were as many crewmembers checking on those leaving the ship as there had been at Mackinac Island, but there was an effort at least.

I had to wonder who would be missing when the ship was ready to sail on to its next port of call. I didn't know who was scheduled to get off at Marquette. Even if I did, I would have no way of knowing if our killer was one of those scheduled to depart there or not.

When we reached the bottom of the gangplank and had just stepped onto the dock, I thought I heard my name called out from somewhere behind me. I turned and looked around, but didn't see anyone on the dock or gangplank that looked like they were trying to get my attention.

It wasn't until I looked up toward the deck above the deck where the gangplank started that I saw one of the ship's officers. He was waving his arm frantically and shouting. I was having a hard time hearing him, so I pointed to my chest as I looked up at him. He nodded his head to indicate that he did want to see me.

I turned and looked at Monica as if to ask her what she wanted me to do. If we had gotten ashore a little sooner, we would have been on our way to an enjoyable day with no knowledge of the fact that I was wanted aboard the ship. But we had been seen, and I had acknowledged that I had seen the officer. This was giving me a bad feeling, a feeling that something was wrong.

The expression on Monica's face indicated that she knew that we would not be making the trip to see the lighthouses. I could see the disappointment in her eyes.

"Do we go back?" I asked, almost hoping that she would say no.

"I think we better," she replied with a sigh.

"Are you sure?"

"Yes. If we don't go back, you will wonder what he wanted all day and so will I. It will ruin our whole day anyway. So we might as well find out what he wants."

I reluctantly nodded in agreement with her assessment of the situation. We turned around. I took her arm and we headed back up the gangplank. When we got to the top, we were met by one of the officers. He had a serious look on his face, and I had to wonder what had happened now.

"I'm sorry to interrupt your day, sir, but this is rather important. Captain Klausen would like to see you as soon as possible," the young officer said.

"Where is the Captain?"

"He's at cabin four-twenty-one."

I looked at the young officer and wondered what was going on. That cabin number sort of sent all kinds of different signals through my head. It took me a minute, but if my memory served me right that was the room that had originally been assigned to Tom. I glanced over at Monica. I got the feeling that she recognized the cabin number, too.

"What's going on there?" I asked as we began to hurry off toward the cabin.

"It seems that they have found another body, sir," he said quietly so no one near us could hear him.

I glanced over at Monica again. This was the second death within two days on this ship. This sure wasn't what I had in mind for our honeymoon. I let out a sigh and pointed toward the stairwell to indicate that the young officer should lead the way.

Monica and I followed the young officer through the stairwells and passageways until we came to the passageway to cabin four-twenty-one. Two members of the ship's crew were standing in front of the cabin. It looked as if they were guarding the cabin door. I noticed that one of them turned and said something to someone inside the cabin, and then quickly turned back around.

As we approached the cabin door, I let go of Monica's arm and quietly suggested that she wait outside. She nodded her head in agreement.

Just as I stepped up to the cabin door, Captain Klausen met me. The look on his face was grim. It crossed my mind that this might be too much to keep the ship on its scheduled course.

"What do you have, Captain?" I asked.

"What we have is another dead body. At least this one is not as messy as the last," he said, his voice low and soft so as not to be overheard by others.

"What do you mean?"

"There's no blood all over the place and the room has not been ransacked. It almost looks as if this man died in his sleep."

"What do you mean by "almost"?"

"At first, we thought that he might have died of a heart attack or stroke, but when the doctor started to check him out he found a small wound at the base of his skull."

"How small a wound?" I asked.

"If it hadn't have been for the spot of blood on the man's pillow, we might never have seen it," the Captain replied.

With that said, the Captain stepped aside and let me in the cabin. I found the doctor sitting on a chair next to the bed. He was looking off into space. I got the feeling that two murders in such a short time were beginning to wear on him.

"You okay, Doc?"

He looked up and shook his head.

"This is getting to be a little much," he said with a sigh.

"I'm sure it is. What do you think is the cause of death?"

"A puncture wound to the base of the skull. Something very small and thin was used, but I can't think of what it might be."

"Let's take a look," I suggested.

The doctor stood up and pulled the blanket away from the body. The man appeared to be in his late thirties or early forties with dark brown hair and some graying around the temples. He was clean shaven and looked to be in fairly good physical shape. From his general appearance there didn't appear to be any reason for him to be dead.

"Do you have some idea when he might have died?" I asked as I continued to look over the body.

"My best guess would be some time last night or very early this morning, but that's only a guess."

"Let's turn him over. I would like to see this wound you found."

Together we rolled him up on his side. There was a small reddish spot on the pillowcase that didn't appear to be made up entirely of blood. There was some kind of clear liquid mixed in with the blood, probably some of the fluid from around the victim's brain.

I quickly found the hole in the back of the man's neck. It was round, not elongated, as one would expect from something like a knife. From the small amount of blood on the pillow, it was clear to me that the wound at the base of the skull had been delivered while the man was lying on his side. It also indicated that it was directed with such precision that it probably killed the man almost instantly.

Based on my experience, the weapon used was most likely an ice pick or some other instrument that was long, thin and very sharp. It could have been inflicted with a long needle such as a hypodermic needle or a long hatpin, or something similar.

I laid the body back down, stood up and began looking around the room. From the looks of the bed and the room, the man never knew what happened. The bed was neat and in good order. There was nothing to indicate any kind of a struggle had taken place.

The room itself had not been ransacked like the other one had. It was in exceptionally good order. Clothes were hung up in the closet, shoes were set side by side on the floor, and a bathrobe was neatly laid over a chair near the bed.

The man's murder was carried out in a neat and orderly manner, and with some degree of skill. I couldn't help but think that his death had all the earmarks of a carefully planned execution. The only question I had was why was he killed?

"Do we know who this guy is?" I asked as I turned and looked at the doctor.

"He is registered as John Parris from Detroit, Michigan."

"Do you know anything about him?

"He listed himself as a businessman, a salesman to be more correctly put. Based on the name of the company he put on his form when he registered for this trip, he sold auto parts of some kind in both the U.S. and Canada."

I looked at Doctor Stillman with some surprise as to how much he seemed to know about the victim.

"How is it you know so much about this man?" I asked.

"I listened to the questions you asked the other night. I looked up all I could find on him and asked the Captain to request a background check on him. We should have it in a few hours," Doctor Stillman said with a slight tone of satisfaction in his voice.

"Good work, Doc. You should work for the police."

"No thank you. I've had more than enough of this. I don't know how you detectives do it day after day," he said.

"Well, it isn't easy. Some deaths seem to bother a person more than others. It's when it's someone young who hasn't had a chance to live life that gets to a guy in a hurry," I said as I remembered my investigation of the death of a young woman just before I left the Milwaukee Police Department.

I took one look around the room again. I had one question that seemed to be bugging me.

"Was this man on the cruise alone?"

"As far as we know. He was the only one registered to this cabin."

"Doc, why would a salesman of auto parts be on a cruise ship alone? Wouldn't it be more profitable for him to travel by some means that would get him from customer to customer quicker?"

"I'm sure you're right. It doesn't make any sense unless he was mixing business with a little pleasure. We get a few business people that do that from time to time," Doctor Stillman explained.

"That's certainly a possibility. Let's see what we can find out about him."

I took another look around the cabin. There wasn't anything I could see that would be of importance at this point. It was time to let the local authorities take over and see what their criminal investigation unit could come up with.

"Have you called the police?"

"Yes. The Captain was on his way to do that when you arrived," Doctor Stillman replied.

"Okay. I don't think there is anything else I can do here. I would like to know what they come up with."

"Sure. By the way, the Captain has already notified the Coast Guard. He thought it was probably a good idea after what happened at Mackinac Island. They're sending someone over to talk to the local police in case there is a connection between the two murders."

"Good thinking. I like it when agencies work together. I'm almost certain that there is a connection, but at this point I don't see it. I'll talk to you later. Keep me posted."

"Will do," he said as I turned and left the cabin.

Monica was still leaning against the wall waiting for me. She straightened up and started toward me when I came out of the cabin. I didn't want to say anything to her where it might be overheard.

"Is it another murder?" she asked in a whisper.

I took her by the arm and started back down the passageway before I answered her.

"Yes, but it doesn't make any sense. The man was murdered, but it was clean and calculated, like a professional execution. This one was nothing like the other."

"Do you think we are dealing with more than one killer?" she asked as we got to the door of our suite.

"I don't know, but there's something strange about this murder. I can't put my finger on it," I said as I unlocked the door to our suite and opened it.

Just as Monica entered our suite, I glanced down the hall. I noticed the old man standing at the corner of the passageway that led to the stairwell. He quickly moved away, but I had already gotten the impression that he had been watching us.

I tend to get a little paranoid when I'm being watched so closely. My first thought was to run down the passageway and have a little heart to heart talk with him, but there were two things stopping me.

The first was Monica. I didn't think it would be a good idea to leave her while I went off on some wild goose chase. I had no idea if there was someone else lurking around just waiting for me to leave her alone.

The second was what would I say to him if I caught him? I had no idea what his interest in us might be.

I turned back to find Monica standing in our suite looking at me. I stepped inside and closed the door. Without giving it a second thought, I locked the door.

CHAPTER THIRTEEN

I turned around after locking the door and found Monica staring at me. The look on Monica's face told me that she was curious about what I had seen in the hall. I knew that she wasn't about to let me get by without telling her.

"What's going on?" Monica asked.

I was hesitant because I didn't want her to worry. On the other hand, we were business partners and lovers, and would soon be married. It would not be right for me to shut her out after going so far together on this case.

"I think you should sit down," I said as I took her by the arm and led her over to the loveseat.

Once we were seated, I told her about seeing the old man in the hall, and that I got the distinct impression that he was more interested in us than what I would consider to be the norm. I also told her everything I could about the death of the second man in the cabin that had originally been assigned to Tom.

When I was finished, she looked at me as if she didn't believe me. Maybe it was because she was having some difficulty understanding the connection between the two deaths since they appeared to be so different. I wasn't sure that I could fully understand it, either.

"Nick, I interrupted you when you had your eyes closed at the table during lunch. You said that you had been thinking about the old man. Do you think that he has something to do with the murders?"

"I don't know. It's certainly possible, but I'm not sure if he has anything to do with anything," I said with a sigh of frustration.

"Well, there is one thing that I do know," she said with a tone of confidence in her voice.

"What's that?" I asked wondering what she was so sure about when I was sure of nothing except that there were two dead men and that they had both been murdered on this ship.

"Every time you get close, maybe a little too close sometimes, to something and can't figure it out, you like to sit back in a quiet place and think about it. You seem to be able to sort things out that way, or maybe it's that you just put things together in your head better. I don't know what it is, but I think this might be a good time for you to do that. Why don't you lay down on the bed, close your eyes while I close the curtains? I'll be quiet so you can think," she suggested.

Her suggestion certainly had merit. I had too many unanswered questions. There was all kinds of information running around in my head and none of it seemed to answer any of the questions. If I could put just a few pieces of the puzzle together, it might help me get a better understanding of the total picture and get me back on track.

"That sounds like a good idea," I admitted.

I laid down on the bed while Monica closed the curtains.

"Would you like me to leave you alone?"

"No. I'd like you to stay here beside me."

Monica smiled as she approached the bed. She laid down, but didn't curl up against me. Instead, she stretched out along side me and remained quiet so I could think.

I closed my eyes and let my mind begin to wander. I mentally sort through all the information that I had firsthand knowledge of. I had to admit that it wasn't much, but it was a place to start.

After I gathered what I knew into my consciousness, I began to sort through it, picking it apart, mentally. I decided to take one person at a time and concentrate on that person until I was finished. Then I would go on to the next. I figured the first one to start with should be the one that I thought was the first one involved, that being Steward James.

It was apparent to me that James was not a very smart young man. He had a rather lengthy arrest record considering his age. However, there was nothing more serious than petty crimes like theft and a couple of attempts at extortion in his record. I had seen nothing in his criminal record that would indicate that he was a violent person.

It crossed my mind that the cruise line didn't do a very good job of checking him out before they hired him. But that was in the past, I had to deal with now.

I tried to picture him and his role with regard to each of the victims. His build gave me the impression that he was not an individual that was inclined toward violence. His build was small without much of a muscular frame. Some people would consider him to be skinny. I doubted that he would have been able to overcome and kill the first victim in such a violent and forceful manner as the evidence indicated.

Then there was his demeanor. His demeanor was that of someone who would rather talk you to death, than raise a fist against you. I felt he was hardly the type to get into a fight with someone as big and strong as the first victim appeared to be. There was also the fact that the killing had been very bloody. James didn't strike me as the type who would allow things to degenerate to that degree without either giving up or running away.

In the case of the second victim, I doubted that James had the skill, or the knowledge of anatomy that it would take to pull off that kind of a murder. It took someone with strength, skill and knowledge of the human anatomy to kill someone using such a calculated and methodical method. Besides the fact that he was not very strong, there was nothing in James's background that would indicate that he had the knowledge, or the skill to kill someone using a well placed ice pick or needle. There was nothing in his actions, or in his criminal record, that pointed to him as the killer in either case.

There was one other thing to consider. The first murder had been so messy that James would not have been able to get himself cleaned up in such a short time.

Mentally eliminating James as the murderer, my thoughts turned to First Officer William Dunbar. He was a well educated man in the mechanics of running a ship, but he was apparently not very smart in the ways of dealing with people.

The fact that he played cards with some of the men, even when he knew that gambling was against the rules, showed me that he was trying to find a way to get to know his men better. It seemed that it was more important to him that they like him. It was obvious to me that it was almost more important to him to be liked by the crew than to be in command of the crew.

Although he had not used very good judgment, I didn't think he had what it took to kill a man without some real serious reason, like to defend himself or a member of his family. Even under those conditions, it didn't seem likely that he would intentionally kill someone. It also occurred to me that he was probably the type of man that would call, or wait for authorities if he did kill someone because it would be in self-defense.

There was the fact that he had taken property that had been stolen and delivered it to a fence, of that there was no doubt. He was not the one who stole it, nor was he the one who had planned it, as far as I could tell. He may be a good First Officer as far as education was concerned, but he didn't strike me as a killer. The look on his face and the color of his skin when he saw Lancaster lying in his own blood told me that he didn't have the stomach for killing.

By mentally eliminating Steward James and First Officer Dunbar as the killers, I had left the door wide open for just about anyone else on the ship. Then it occurred to me, that there was one other that it might not be a bad idea to check out. His name was Higgins, the old man that seemed to show up at the most unlikely times.

I realized that I had no real knowledge of this man, Higgins. The more I thought about him, the more I felt it would be a good idea to get a background check on him. If nothing showed up, it would eliminate him as a possible suspect and no harm done.

As I laid there with my eyes closed, I once again began to envision Mr. Higgins in my mind's eye. I mentally studied every detail of him that I could remember. The first thing that came to mind was his walk. I had been aware of it from the very first time that I saw him. He didn't walk like a man as old as he appeared to be. He walked with the straight back and firm stride of someone who had confidence in himself, and his steps were quick. His stride was fairly long for a man of his apparent age.

The next thing that I remembered was how he had reacted when he accidentally bumped into Tom. I remembered that he had hardly touched Tom as they passed in the passageway. Yet, he reached for his arm as if to protect it from further harm. Even the look on his face indicated that it had hurt just to brush against Tom.

I suddenly remembered something else that should not have slipped by me. The report we got from the Coast Guard indicated that there were two types of blood found at the scene of the first murder. That meant that two people had been injured during the fight, the one who was dead and the one who had done the killing. The one who had done the killing had probably been hurt while trying to kill the first one. I hadn't remembered either James or Dunbar showing any signs of an injury.

The fact that Higgins bumped into Tom and grabbed his arm as if it hurt him was not proof that he was the other man. But the fact that he was an older man didn't count him out, either. I decided that I would try to get a background check on him as soon as possible. In the meantime I would see if I could find out why his arm hurt him. The place to start was to ask Doctor Stillman if anyone on board had come to him for the treatment of a cut or laceration. If he had not been treated for a cut, it would not eliminate him as one of my suspects. It may have been a case of him taking care of his injury by himself, or with the help of someone else.

* * * *

Just as I was about to open my eyes, I heard a knock on the door. I glanced over at Monica to find that she was looking at me. The look on her face told me that she was curious to know who was at our door this time, but wasn't sure if I was ready to get up.

I swung my feet off the side of the bed, got up and walked to the door. A quick glance back at Monica told me that she was ready for me to open the door. I reached out and turned the knob.

As the door opened, I could see one of the ship's officers standing in the passageway. I wasn't sure if someone else had been killed, or if he simply had information for me.

"Mr. McCord, the Captain asked me to deliver this to you as soon as possible."

I reached out and took the large envelope. I thanked the officer and closed the door.

"We have another envelope," I said as I held it up for Monica to see.

As I walked back across the room toward Monica, I noticed that she was staring at the envelope. I sat down on the edge of the bed beside her and began opening the envelope.

The first thing I found was a report on one Mr. John Parris. I carefully read the report. I had to admit it was not what I had suspected. The fact that he was what he proclaimed to be set me back for just a moment. I guess I had expected something else. He was a salesman for an auto parts company out of Detroit, Michigan. The report showed that he had no criminal record, not even a traffic ticket. A footnote explained that he was on the cruise as part of a reward for his salesmanship, and it had been paid for by the company that employed him.

Now I was really confused. Why had this man been killed? What did he have, or what did someone think he had, that made it was necessary to kill him? What did he know, or what did someone think he knew? Getting this report certainly caused more questions than it answered.

"What's the matter," Monica asked, seeing the look on my face as I stared off into space.

"I can see no reason for Mr. Parris's murder," I replied as I handed her the report.

I watched Monica as she read the report. I could see the confused look on her face. She was wondering the same thing.

"I don't understand," she said as she looked at me, the look on her face showing that she did not understand this man's death any more than I did.

"I don't either."

"Is there anything else in the envelope?" she asked as she glanced at it.

I pulled the envelope open and looked inside. Down deep in the bottom of it were two pieces of paper that were neatly folded together. I reached in, pulled them out and unfolded them, one at a time. I looked at the first one very carefully.

The first piece of paper was a fax from A-1 Security, Inc. It stated that Frank Wright had not been to work for the past four or five days, but that he had called in sick with the flu.

I was not surprised that Frank Wright had called in sick. The time frame of his sickness seemed to correspond perfectly with the timing of the robberies. I was sure that the robberies would not have taken place more than a couple of days before the ship left Chicago, probably only the day before. Calling in sick would give him a couple of days head start before anyone would get suspicious.

Included with the fax from A-1 Security, Inc. was a physical description of Frank Wright. The most interesting part of the description of Wright was that it didn't even come close to anyone remotely looking like Lancaster. Lancaster was a good size man, while Wright was short and slim. Yet, that was not the most interesting part of the note. There was a big difference in their ages as well. Nothing about the two could be matched up, not even the color of their hair.

The second piece of paper was a fax from the Wisconsin prison that Lancaster had been in before his release. It listed all the known people that had been in contact with our first murder victim, namely William F. Lancaster. I began to scan the list of people that Lancaster was known to have had contact with during the last three to four months that he was incarcerated. The list was broken down into several sections.

The first section contained just a few names of people who had visited him from the outside. On that list was the name, Frank Wright. I found it interesting that Frank Wright would have listed his real name when he visited Lancaster in prison, but then no one ever said that crooks were smart, except for the crooks themselves. He may have thought that he would be long gone before anyone discovered the connection between them.

The report indicated that Wright had visited Lancaster on several occasions, most of them over the past month to a month and a half. That information gave us our connection between Wright and Lancaster, but even with Wright's help I still didn't think that Lancaster had the knowledge to pull off that kind of heist.

"It seems that the police should be looking for our Mr. Frank Wright. I seriously doubt that they will find him alive," I said as I looked up at Monica.

I began to scan the list of people who called Lancaster from outside the prison. There again I found several calls from Frank Wright. The interesting thing was that Lancaster received no other calls. That proved to be disappointing. I was hoping to get a lead on who the mastermind was. I certainly didn't think it was Lancaster, and I seriously doubted that it was Wright.

It wasn't until I got to the list of inmates that were housed in the same cellblock as Lancaster that things began to look up. One name literally jumped off the page at me as if it had been printed in bold red print.

"Well, I'll be damned."

"What did you find?" Monica asked, a little surprised at my reaction.

"It seems that an old friend of ours might be involved in all this," I said as I looked up at Monica.

"Who's that?" she asked impatiently.

"Andrew Thorndike," I said with a smile.

"Thorndike, Andrew Thorndike from England?" she asked, the expression on her face showing that she could hardly believe me.

"Yes. One and the same," I replied almost not believing it myself.

"But he's supposed to be in jail."

"He is as far as I know."

"Is it possible that he is out of jail?" Monica asked.

"I wouldn't think so. He was sent up for life without parole. He should still be there."

"You mean that you think there's a possibility that he might be out of jail?" she asked.

"I mean I don't know. Even if he is in jail, it wouldn't be the first time that a heist was planned, coordinated and carried out while the leader was behind bars. He's certainly smart enough to plan it from jail."

"Are you saying that Thorndike planned and coordinated the robberies while in jail? That doesn't sound like him."

"You're right, it doesn't. But it would not be the first time that a thief changed his MO, either," I replied as an idea came to me.

The first time I ran into Thorndike, he was after the jewelry that had been stolen by one of his relatives, namely Captain Bartholomew Samuelson. I had been the one that prevented him from getting the jewelry last time. I only hoped that I could stop him again.

"What are you thinking?" Monica asked.

"I was wondering about Thorndike," I replied without going any further.

Monica didn't say anything for a while. I don't know what she was thinking, but I was thinking about Thorndike. The more I thought about him, the more things seemed to take shape in my head.

He had tried to get the treasure that his relative, Captain Samuelson, had stolen during his pirating activities on the Great Lakes. Now all of a sudden, we have two robberies involving the same treasure, or at least part of the same treasure. Why? Who would want just that part of a much bigger treasure? What was in the jewelry stolen that made him want just that when there was so much else to be had that would bring him the same amount of money without drawing so much attention?

"What are you thinking, Nick?" Monica finally asked.

"I'm thinking we need a few questions answered and we need them answered as quickly as possible. For one thing, we need to know everything that was stolen."

"We have the lists," Monica reminded me.

"I mean everything else, anything that was not part of the Samuelson Collection."

"That shouldn't be a big deal. Both of the museums have a detailed list of everything that they have."

"We need to know how much contact Thorndike would have had with Lancaster. I should be able to get that information by making a phone call to the prison."

"We can do that from here," Monica said as she nodded her head in agreement.

"I also need to find out who this Higgins fella is. And I need to find out if Thorndike is still in prison."

"We can do all that from here."

She was right. I picked up the phone and asked the ship's operator for an outside line. I called the local operator for the number of the prison where Lancaster had been incarcerated. The operator gave me the number and then connected me to the warden's office at the prison.

CHAPTER FOURTEEN

A woman with a very pleasant and cheery voice answered the phone at the prison. Upon my request to speak to the warden, she immediately put me through.

"This is Warden Crockett."

"Mr. Crockett, my name is Nick McCord."

"Good Morning, Detective McCord. I have heard of you, or more correctly put, I have seen your name on several of the police reports of people who are currently residents here. What can I do for you?

"Well, first of all I'm no longer with the Milwaukee Police Department."

"Oh, I didn't know that. Well, it doesn't matter. How might I help you?"

"I'm currently working on a murder case for Great Lakes Cruise Line. I need a little information from you."

"Certainly. What is it you need?"

"You had an inmate by the name of William F. Lancaster."

"Yes, we did, but he has been released," the warden said interrupting me. "He was released about two weeks ago."

"I know that he was released, but that's beside the point."

"He hasn't committed another crime already, has he?"

"Well, not that I can prove. In fact, he's dead."

"Dead?"

"Yes."

"What was the cause of his death?"

"He was murdered, but I'm not interested in him at the moment. What I want to know is can you tell me how much contact he might have had with one of your other inmates, namely Andrew Thorndike?"

"Oh, yes. That Thorndike is a strange one."

"Yes, I know."

"He has mentioned you on several occasions. And I might add, not in the most flattering of terms," Warden Crockett said with a slight chuckle in his voice. "He is still mad at you for getting him put behind bars."

"I'm sure he is."

"By the way, did you know that he escaped?"

That was one piece of news that came as a big surprise. I had thought it was a possibility, but really didn't believe that in this day and age it was easy to escape from such a modern prison. It also gave me a whole new line of questions for the Warden.

"No, I didn't know that he had escaped. When did that happen? I need to know how long ago as close as you can come."

"Six days ago today."

"You're sure?"

"Very. It was one of the worst days of my life. He is the only inmate to ever escape since I've been warden, and I've been the warden here for the past fourteen years," the sound of his voice showing how angry he was over it.

"How did he get out?"

"It was one of the oldest tricks in the book. He escaped while we were removing a prisoner who died during the night."

The warden went on to explain that the prisoner in the cell next to Thorndike's had died during the night.

"When the guard discovered the dead inmate during his routine rounds, he had left the cell door open. He called for the prison doctor.

"After the prison doctor had certified that the inmate was dead, the guard left the cell doors unsecured in that section of the cellblock while he went to get help to remove the body. The guard apparently didn't think it was necessary to lock the cell doors, as the rest of the inmates in that section of the cellblock were asleep, so he thought," he continued.

"It was not clear just how it all happened, but they think that Thorndike changed places with the dead inmate after he had been put in a body bag and while the guard went for a gurney to wheel him out. The body bag was taken to a room near one of the service gates where it was picked up by a local funeral home, which would explain how he got outside the walls of the prison.

"I can tell you that there are a couple of guards that are looking at some very stiff disciplinary action," Warden Crockett said angrily. "If they had done their job like they were supposed to, Thorndike would still be here."

"I'm sure," I replied.

"What is it you wanted to know about Thorndike?" the warden asked, suddenly realizing that he had not answered my question.

"Did Thorndike have any contact with Lancaster?"

"Sure. They were on the same cellblock. They went to exercise in the courtyard at the same time every day."

"Then they knew each other pretty well?"

"I'm sure they did. They spent a lot of time playing chess. I think Thorndike taught Lancaster how to play. Lancaster never got very good at it, by the way."

"I think that's all I need for now."

"I hope I was of some help."

"You have been a great deal of help. By the way, what was the name of the inmate in the cell next to Thorndike. The one that died?" I asked on a hunch.

"His name was Higgins, Henry Howard Higgins. Why, is it important?"

"No, not really. Can you tell me what he was in prison for?"

"Higgins?" he asked.

"Yes."

"He killed his wife and her lover some thirty years ago."

"Then this Higgins fella was not a young man."

"No. He was seventy-two."

"Thanks for the information. You have been very helpful. Can you tell me what was the cause of Higgins' death?"

"He died of natural causes. A massive stroke, I think the doctor said. He had a history of medical problems including a bad heart."

"Might I make a suggestion?"

"Sure."

"You might want to have a talk with the doctor who examined him. You might have him examine the back of Higgins' neck for a small puncture wound at or near the base of the skull. You may find that he didn't die of natural causes."

"What are you saying?"

I could hear the concern in his voice. It would not go over very well if the warden found out that Thorndike had killed an inmate in order to escape.

"Take a look. I think he might have been killed so that Thorndike had a way to escape."

"I'll have it looked into, right away," the warden assured me.

"Thanks for the help."

"Like I said, you can call anytime. Glad to help. Since you seem to know so much about Thorndike, you don't know where we can find him, do you?" he asked with a slight chuckle in his voice.

"Not right at the moment. But if I find him, I'll be sure to send him back to you."

"You do that. You do that. I'd like nothing more than to have him back here."

"I'm sure."

As I hung up the phone, my thoughts were still of Higgins. If he was murdered in his cell, and Thorndike had used that opportunity to escape; then it seemed to make sense that the man on the ship claiming to be Higgins was really Thorndike. That could explain why Tom thought he recognized him.

If Higgins was Thorndike, even though he had changed his appearance, he could not hide everything about himself. There would always be those little quirks that were definitely Thorndike, and they would give him away if anyone recognized them. The problem was that they were often so subtle that they were overlooked unless someone knew him fairly well and was looking for them.

"What's going on?" Monica asked disturbing my thoughts.

"It appears that Thorndike has escaped from prison. I think that there is a very good chance that he is posing as Higgins," I said.

"You mean that Higgins, the old man, is really Thorndike?"

"I don't know, but if my gut feeling is right, it would appear so."

"That would explain why he has been watching us so closely, don't you think?"

"I'm sure you're right."

I knew that there were a lot of Higginses in this world. It would not do me any good to go up to him and embarrass him if he was not who I was beginning to think he was. But on the other hand, it would not help any if I did nothing and he got away. I knew him to be a hard, cold man who could kill without even thinking twice about it.

"What do we do now?" Monica asked.

"I would like a little more time to think," I replied.

As I laid back down on the bed, Monica curled up beside me. This time she laid her hand on my chest while resting her head on my shoulder.

I remembered what the warden had said about the way Thorndike had talked about me. It was clear that he would not hesitate to kill me if he got the chance. I also

remembered what he had to say about me at his trial. He had threatened to kill me. He was a man who would do whatever he said he would if given even the slightest opportunity. With him out of jail, there was always the chance that he would try to find me. And if I remembered his threat, he had included Monica in it.

Now I really had something to think about. It became apparent that Monica was in as much danger as I was if it turned out that Higgins was really Thorndike. That thought made me draw Monica up closer against me. Thorndike would get at me any way he could, and that would include hurting Monica.

"What's the matter?" she asked as she raised her head up off my shoulder.

I knew it would do no good to lie to her. She would know that something was not right. She also had the right to know that her life might be in danger.

I began by letting her know what was on my mind. If Thorndike had killed Higgins as I thought he had, then there was a very distinct possibility that the Higgins on board this ship was Thorndike. If he was Thorndike, then neither Monica nor I were safe. We were both targets.

"Do you think Thorndike is aboard this ship?" Monica asked.

"I don't know, but we can't take any chances. We have to believe that he is. Otherwise, we leave ourselves vulnerable. We have to stay alert at all times."

"If Thorndike knows we're on this ship, why hasn't he tried to kill us already? He's had the opportunity to at least try."

"I don't know. Maybe he's willing to give up the opportunity to kill us for the chance to escape with his jewelry. As long as he believes that we have not recognized him, he probably feels he has a chance to get away with the jewelry. I think he is more interested in escaping with his treasure than in getting even with us for catching him the first time, at least for now. That could easily change if he thinks we might recognize him and spoil his plans.

"What are you going to do?"

"I think the first thing that I have to do is find out as much about Higgins, the one on this ship, as I can, and as fast as I can."

"You can request a criminal record on him, can't you?"

"Sure, but I already know what his criminal record will say. I need to know if the Higgins on this ship is Thorndike or someone else, and I need to know it fast."

"You could ask the Captain for what he has on him. If his full name is the same as the Higgins that died, then there's a very good chance that he is really Thorndike," she explained.

There was no doubt that Monica's idea was a good one. I had thought of that already, but I wanted more than just a match up of names. I needed some sort of proof. There was also the possibility that he might have changed his first name or middle name, which would make it just that much harder to verify that it was Thorndike.

Whatever we found out, I was not about to let Monica out of my sight. The risk was too great. I felt I knew Thorndike well enough to know that if he couldn't get to me, he would go after the one person in my life that I cared about the most, Monica.

I held her close to me as I thought about what I was going to do. It seemed the more I held onto her, the more she held onto me.

"Nick?"

"Yeah?"

"I love you," she whispered.

I turned and looked into those cobalt blue eyes. I could see her love for me in them, and I knew that I loved her.

"I love you, too," I said as I leaned down and kissed her.

Suddenly, in the middle of our kiss, an idea hit me. It was so obvious that I couldn't understand why I hadn't thought of it before. There was one person who might be able to tell me if the old man on the ship was Thorndike.

"You remember when Tom said that he thought he knew the old man in the restaurant?"

"Yes. Sure."

"I think the reason he thought he recognized the old man was because he did. Well, he sort of recognized him. There was something about the old man that struck a cord in Tom's memory."

"You're saying there was something about that old man that rang a bell in Tom's head, something he was aware of, but couldn't place where he had seen it before?" Monica asked.

"Yeah. Something like that."

"You think that this is why Tom was so sure that he recognized the old man?"

"Yes. Tom recognized the old man because he had seen him before, but he looks different now. And I think that Tom might be able to tell us if this guy Higgins is really Thorndike."

"How? How could he do that if he hasn't already recognized him?"

"I think if we plant the idea that the old man is actually Thorndike, Tom might be able to put it together."

"I don't know," she replied somewhat skeptical of my idea. "Wouldn't planting the idea in Tom's head convince Tom that he is Thorndike?

"Possibly, but I don't think so. You have to remember that Tom was around him for almost three months before we arrived at the lodge. In that time he would have picked up on some of Thorndike's little quirks, those little movements and gestures or habits that are so hard to break in a short period of time. Some of them Tom might not even realize he knows. We were around him for only three days or so, and didn't see much of him even then," I added.

"What kind of things would Tom know about?" Monica asked.

"Things like the way he holds his silverware when he eats. Maybe he holds his fork in his left hand while he cuts his meat and then eats it without putting down his knife or shifting his fork to his right hand. Maybe the fact that he is left handed rather than right handed. Maybe he holds his little finger out when he sips his hot coffee or tea. Maybe something about the way he walks that's different. I don't know, but there has to be something he does or doesn't do that would set him apart from others."

I knew I was reaching at straws, but I didn't really have anything else to go on. I had to find out if it was Thorndike that we were dealing with on the ship.

"Do you think Tom would remember things like that?"

"I don't know, but somewhere down deep in his brain, I'd be willing to bet that Tom will see something about this old man that reminds him of Thorndike."

"When do we talk to Tom about it?"

"As soon as they get back from their tour."

"What do we do now?"

"I think it would be a good idea if we got in touch with the Captain and found out how much he knows about our Mr. Higgins," I said.

"Okay," Monica replied, then rolled away from me so that I could sit up and call the Captain.

I placed my call to the ship's operator and was immediately transferred to the bridge. Captain Klausen answered the phone.

"This is Captain Klausen."

"Captain, this is Nick McCord."

"Yes, Mr. McCord. What can I do for you?"

"I would like to get a little information on one of your passengers.

"Which one?"

"Mr. Higgins."

155

"Let me check our roster. Please hold on a moment," he said, and then there was silence.

I looked over at Monica while I waited impatiently for the Captain to come back on the line. The look on her face told me that she was as impatient as I was to find out what was going on.

"Mr. McCord?"

"Yes."

"I have two Higgins' listed on the roster, or should I say three."

"Three?"

"Yes. There is a Mr. and Mrs. Oliver Higgins. He is listed as being from Toronto, Ontario. There is also a Mr. Harvey W. Higgins. He is also listed as being from Ontario, but he is from Thunder Bay."

"It has to be Harvey. The one I'm interested in is traveling alone. How old would you say this Harvey is?"

"It appears that he is in his mid-to-late forties.

"Are you sure?"

"Yes. Ah, this is interesting," the Captain said, the tone of his voice suddenly changing indicating that he had found something that was unusual.

"What's interesting, Captain?"

"It seems that there is a note here on the roster. It's a request that Mrs. Oliver Higgins not be disturbed as she is ill."

"Really?"

That bit of information grabbed my attention very quickly.

"Yes. It seems that she is on her way back to Canada for treatment of some sort of illness."

"Captain, doesn't it seem a little strange that someone would take a cruise ship to go to Canada when it is highly unlikely that she would be able to enjoy such a trip? Especially since she is ill and apparently confined to her cabin?"

"Well, yes. It does seem a little strange," the Captain agreed.

"And didn't you say that they are from Toronto?"

"Yes," he replied.

"This boat doesn't go to Toronto."

"You're right. It doesn't."

"Captain, how old is Mr. Oliver Higgins?"

"I don't really know, but I would guess that he is in his late sixties, maybe early seventies. Why? Is that important?"

"It may be. Just out of curiosity, has anyone actually seen Mrs. Oliver Higgins?"

"I don't know. I haven't, but then I often don't see all the passengers in the first couple of days of a cruise. I'll check around. If anyone has seen her, it would be one of the stewards. It appears that she has been having her meals taken to her room."

"Would you let me know what you find out?"

"Certainly," he replied.

"Thank you, Captain. You've been a great deal of help."

"You're welcome."

I couldn't help but smile as I hung up the phone. The Captain didn't know it, but he had told me more than he realized.

CHAPTER FIFTEEN

"Well, are you going to tell me what it is that you find so amusing?" Monica asked.

"Not so much funny as it is interesting. The Captain doesn't know it, but he just told me that Thorndike is on this ship. He is posing as Mr. Oliver Higgins, the old man."

"You figured that out talking to the Captain?"

"Yes."

"What makes you so sure?"

"Oliver Higgins is an old man who is on this ship with his ailing wife."

"But Thorndike doesn't have a wife."

"Right. But if you remember, he didn't have one at the lodge, either. Well, at least he didn't have one after he and his sister had killed the prostitute he was parading around as his wife."

"That's right," she said as she remembered what had happened at the lodge.

"Do you remember what he did so no one would suspect anything when his so called wife didn't come down to the dining room for meals?"

"Yes. He said she was sick and took her meals to her in their room," Monica said with a grin.

"He's doing it again. He is having meals sent to his cabin for his ailing wife," I said, sure of myself.

"Do you think he knows we are on to him?"

"No. I seriously doubt it. If Thorndike was sure that we knew he was on the ship, he would have made some attempt to kill us before we could let the authorities know," I said, then I stopped suddenly as a thought passed through my mind.

I began to think about Tom and Mr. Parris, the second man to be murdered. If Thorndike realized that we knew he was aboard the ship, he would try to kill us, of that I had no doubt. I then began to put my thoughts together in what I thought was some semblance of logical order. The more I thought about it, the more I began to think that the murder of Mr. Parris actually did make some sense.

"Monica, I think I know why Mr. Parris was murdered."

"You do? Why?"

"Do you remember what cabin Tom was originally assigned to on the ship?"

Monica's mouth fell open as she began to realize what was going through my head. I gave her a minute to let the idea soak in.

"Tom was assigned to the same cabin that Mr. Parris was in. I knew that, but I didn't put it together," she said.

"That's right. I knew it, too, but I didn't put it together until now, either. This may be reaching a bit, but I think Mr. Parris was mistaken for Tom in the darkness of the cabin. He was killed for no other reason than he happened to be in the cabin that Tom should have been in."

"It could have been Tom in that cabin," Monica said as she realized how close Tom may have come to being murdered.

"Yes. And my guess is our killer was sure that Tom was supposed to be in that cabin. Do you remember what Mr. Parris looked like?"

"No, not really. I'm not sure that I ever saw him," Monica replied after thinking about it.

"He was about the same build as Tom. His hair was dark and combed not so much different than Tom combs his. It would be easy for someone to mistake them in the dark, especially if he didn't know either of them very well."

"But wouldn't he know that Tom had been moved to a cabin on the other side of the ship?"

"He might have if he had bothered to check the register of passengers. My guess is he never checked it to make sure that Tom was still in that cabin. What reason would he have to check it? He had seen Tom go into that cabin."

"But didn't Pamela say that the old man saw them go into her cabin?"

"Not really. She said that he saw them at her door. And remember, Tom said that he saw the old man when he went into Mr. Parris' cabin to pick up his briefcase that had been left there when he changed cabins.

"I know this is reaching a bit, but I think Thorndike was trying to kill Tom before he had a chance to remember who he is, and before Tom had a chance to tell me that the old man is really Thorndike."

"Why would Thorndike, wanted for escaping from prison, kill Mr. Parris? Wouldn't it cause a great deal of problems for him? It certainly would draw attention to him from the police or at least the Coast Guard."

"You're right about that, but you have to remember that he thought he was killing Tom. I believe that Thorndike is arrogant enough to think that he can get away with using his disguise. Plus, Higgins would have no connection to Tom and would probably be overlooked as a suspect."

"Don't you think you're stretching it a bit?" Monica asked, not sure that anyone had that much confidence in himself.

"You might be right, but I don't remember ever meeting anyone that was as confident in himself as Thorndike, confident to the point of arrogance. I believe that he was so convinced that no matter what, he would be successful in anything he attempted to do. I think he was so sure of himself and his ability that he had convinced himself that he was smarter than anyone and that he would never get caught."

"But he did get caught. You caught him, remember?" Monica said with a grin.

"Yes, I did, but I'm sure that in his mind he thought of it as only a minor setback to his overall plans. His plans were to steal the jewelry and get it back to England where he could sell it off and live happily ever after."

"Maybe, but he still got caught," Monica added.

"True. I think when Tom went up to him in the restaurant, Thorndike got scared. He was afraid that given time Tom would figure out who he was. If Tom did and told me about it, the police would be down on him before he could make his escape to England.

"It makes perfect sense to eliminate any clogs in the plans. Tom could very well prove to be the fly in his ointment, so to speak," I said.

"Do you really think it's that simple?" Monica asked.

"Yes," I replied after giving it some more thought. "If Tom had not made contact with him in the restaurant, I believe that Mr. Parris would still be alive. I don't think that even Thorndike would go to such extremes unless he thought that if he didn't, it would cause his plans to fail. Thorndike doesn't handle failure very well. I believe he will do anything to prevent his plan from failing, and I mean anything."

"I see your point," Monica agreed with some reluctance. "But do you really think that Tom would have recognized Higgins as Thorndike?"

"Yes. I do. Sooner or later Tom would have figured it out. But it doesn't matter what we think. What matters is what Thorndike thinks. If Higgins is Thorndike, he might think that given time and seeing him around the ship often enough, Tom would eventually put two and two together and figure out who he really is."

Monica sat there looking at me as if she was trying to figure out if I might have a point. It wasn't until her eyes got big that I realized that she had come up with something that I might have overlooked.

"What's on your mind, Honey?"

"Here is something you might want to think about. Tom still doesn't know that Higgins is really Thorndike, right?" she asked.

"Right," I replied wondering what Monica was getting at.

"What's going to happen when Thorndike finds out that Tom is alive and still a threat to him? Wouldn't he make another attempt to kill Tom?"

"I'm sure he would," I said as what she was telling soaked in. "He can't risk being found out now."

"Then we have to find Tom and tell him what we know, or at least what we suspect," Monica said. "Tom has a right to know that his life may be in danger."

"I agree. I think we need to warn Pamela, too."

"Yes. If Tom is sleeping with her, she's in as much danger of getting killed as Tom is."

"You're right about that."

"One other thing, did Thorndike leave the ship today?" Monica asked.

"I don't know, but I think we had better be finding out."

I reached over and picked up the phone. I got the ship's operator and asked for the officer who was checking people on and off the ship. She transferred my call immediately.

"This is Officer Wilcox. How may I help you?"

"This is Nick McCord. Are you checking people on and off the ship?"

"Yes, sir."

"Can you tell me if Mr. Oliver Higgins went ashore?"

"Let me check the list, sir," he said.

I waited nervously while he checked. It seemed to me that it was taking him an unreasonable amount of time to find out what I needed to know now.

"Mr. McCord, I show that Mr. Oliver Higgins did go ashore early this morning with a woman. I believe it was his wife."

"What?"

"Yes, sir. He left the ship with several people all at the same time. I marked it down on the list as him leaving the ship with his wife."

"Tell me, what did the woman look like?"

"Let me think. She was a very well dressed woman in her sixties, I would guess. She had gray hair, was rather short and stocky, and she walked rather slowly. She had her arm in his and they were chatting as they walked down the gangplank together. They walked rather slowly, I might add."

"Thank you," I said.

It took me a minute to put two and two together. It was clear to me that she was not his wife, but then I knew that he didn't have a wife. I was convinced that he had taken the woman by the arm to help her down the gangplank with the intent of making it look like he was helping his wife. It was a trick that was as old as time itself, but it had apparently worked. Now comes the real question, where did he go?

I turned and looked at Monica as I hung up the phone. She had been listening to my end of the conversation, but had not heard the officer's part.

"He left the ship with a woman on his arm a few hours ago," I said to Monica.

"With a woman?"

"Yeah, but I think it was just a lady that he helped down the gangplank for the purpose of fooling the officer into thinking it was his wife."

"I think we should try to find Tom and Pamela before it's too late," Monica said, the tone of her voice and the look in her eyes showing that she was worried that it might already be too late.

"Come on. We're going ashore." I said as I stood up.

Monica and I got ready to go ashore in very short order.

* * * *

We left the ship and headed for the shop where the "Anatomy of A Murder" tours begin. We found out that it was a self-guided tour where you follow the directions in a brochure that took you to different locations where the nineteen fifty-nine movie was made. I looked at the brochure and then looked down the street.

"I wonder where they would be by now." Monica asked.

"I don't know. I have no idea if they stuck with the directions in the tour brochure, or if they skipped around."

"They may have gone off to do something else, too," she added.

I reviewed the brochure to get some idea of how long it would take to cover the complete tour. It said on the brochure that the tour took two to three hours, depending on how much time was spent at each stop and how fast one walked. I looked at my watch. It had been well over two hours since they had left the ship.

"They've been gone a long time. They could have completed the tour and gone on to something else by now," I said as I started to get a little worried about them.

"Maybe we should start at the end of the tour and work backwards. If they haven't finished the tour, we stand a better chance of finding them quicker," Monica suggested.

"Good idea."

Monica and I hurried to the last location in the self-guided tour brochure. We didn't waste time with what there was to see, we looked for Tom and Pamela. When we didn't find them, we went on. By the time we were half way through the tour, we realized that we must have missed them.

We stopped at a street corner and looked around. There were several people from the ship on the street, but we had not bothered to ask if they had seen Tom and Pamela. The chance that they would know who we were talking about was slim at best.

"Look," Monica said as she pointed across the street to a couple coming out of a gift shop.

"I don't see them," I said, expecting to see Tom and Pamela.

"No, it's not them. The old couple coming out of the gift shop. I saw them talking to Tom and Pamela just before we caught up with them for dinner the other night. If they remember them, they might know where they went."

I doubted that they would be able to help, but at this point it was worth a try. After all, we didn't have any better options.

"Okay," I said as I took Monica by the arm.

We hurried across the street and caught up with the couple as they were about to head into another gift shop.

"Excuse us, please," Monica said.

"Yes, what is it," the man said, the look in his eyes showing that he was being cautious.

"We are looking for a young couple from the cruise ship. I saw you talking to them the other night at dinner. Do you happen to know where they might have gone?"

"I don't think we know who you are?" the man said.

"We are on the same cruise ship as you. The couple we are looking for are friends of ours. We need to get in touch with them," I said.

"I know who these people are," the woman said with a pleasant smile. "You're the couple that is going to get married on the ship,"

"Yes, that's right," Monica replied with one of her disarming smiles.

"They're looking for Tom and Pamela, dear," the woman said to her husband.

"Oh. Well, they were on the "Anatomy of A Murder" tour the last time we saw them."

"Yes, we know that. What we need to know is do you happen to know where they were going from there?" I asked.

"I don't think we can help you," the man said after he thought a moment.

"Wait, I think I heard them say that they were going to the Marquette Lighthouse. Now mind you, I'm not real sure about that," the woman said.

"Thank you, thank you very much," I said.

The old couple nodded, then turned and went into the gift shop. I turned and looked at Monica only to find her looking at me. I could see that we had no better information to go on, so I believed that our next stop should be the Marquette Lighthouse.

"Shall we get a cab and go to the lighthouse?" Monica asked.

"Unless you have a better idea," I said.

"I don't," she replied.

I flagged down a cab. I asked the driver to hurry out to the Marquette Lighthouse. It wasn't a very long ride, but it seemed like it took forever.

* * * *

As I got out of the cab, I immediately began looking around. The red brick lighthouse was impressive, but it was not what I was interested in. The one thing I did notice was that there were not very many people around.

As I reached out a hand to Monica, I happened to glance over the top of the cab. I noticed that there were two local police cars parked near the walkway to the lighthouse. My first thought was that the worst had already happened. That Thorndike had caught up with Tom and Pamela before we did.

"What's the matter?" Monica asked.

I looked at her. She must have seen the worried look on my face. I glanced back at the police cars again before saying anything.

"I just hope that we are not too late."

Monica turned and looked toward the police cars. I could hear her breath catch.

"Come on," I said as I took her arm.

We walked at a pretty good pace toward the lighthouse. All the time I was hoping for the best, but expecting the worst. As we came around the corner on the path to the lighthouse, we saw several police officers gathered around what looked like a body covered with a sheet. There appeared to be only one body.

One of the officers was talking to a man in a sport coat. As he talked, he looked up. I also looked up. It became clear that the person under the sheet had fallen from the lighthouse. I had to wonder if the person under the sheet lost his balance and fell, or if he had been pushed.

"Oh, my God," Monica said as she stopped suddenly and covered her mouth.

I turned in front of her and took her in my arms. She buried her head in my shoulder. I could feel her body tremble against me.

"Honey, it might not be either of them," I said softly, not sure if I believed what I was saying myself.

I could feel her respond to my statement. Her breathing seemed to become more normal and the tension in her body lessened. She slowly lifted her head off my shoulder and looked up at me.

"I'm sorry," she whispered.

"It's okay."

I took a quick look around. I noticed a bench off to the side of the path under a large oak tree.

"Come over here," I said as I gently guided her toward the bench. "I want you to sit down here while I try to find out who is under the sheet."

She looked up at me as if she didn't want me to leave her, not even for one minute.

"Sit here. I'll be right back," I said as I leaned close and kissed her lightly on the forehead.

I turned and started toward the officers. As I walked toward them, I glanced back to see if Monica was all right. She was watching me, apparently looking for some reassurance that everything was going to be all right.

As I approached the officers, one of them looked toward me. The closer I got, the more interested in me he seemed to become. When I got close, he stepped up in front of me.

"Can I help you, sir?" he asked.

"My name is Nick McCord. I'm a private investigator."

"We have enough to do without you interfering with our investigation," the young officer said rather sharply.

"I'm not interested in interfering with your investigation. I'm only interested in who is under that sheet."

"Why do you want to know that? You working for some newspaper?"

"No. I'm missing a friend who I believe came out here to the lighthouse. I want to know if you have him lying under that sheet," I replied, not happy with the lack of cooperation I was getting from the officer; nor was I very happy with his adversarial attitude.

"This 'friend' of yours, is he wanted for something?"

"No, he is not. Listen, I'm just looking for a friend. If you find it so difficult to help me, maybe you would be so kind as to tell the detective assigned to this case that I would like to speak with him. He's standing right over there," I said as I pointed at him.

"Why should I?" the young officer asked, the tone in his voice letting me know that he seemed to think that he had all the authority in the world.

"Because it might prove rather embarrassing for you, to say nothing of how you will look to your boss, if you don't," I replied, the tone of my voice letting him know that I was not going to be intimidated by the young rookie flexing his badge at me. I'd seen officers like him before and it usually got them into trouble.

He didn't say anything for a moment or two as he looked at me. I got the impression that he was trying to decide if I might know something that the lead detective would want to know.

"Wait here," he said, then turned and started to walk away.

"Good decision," I said to his back.

CHAPTER SIXTEEN

I watched as the young police officer walked toward the man in a light gray sport coat. They talked for a moment or two before the man in the sport coat turned and looked toward me. He said something to the young officer that I could not hear, and then waited for him to respond. After the young officer talked to him again, I saw the man in the sport coat nod and start toward me.

As he walked, I could see the midday sun shine off the detective's badge that was hanging from the breast pocket of his sport coat. The detective was probably in his mid-forties with slightly graying hair. He looked as if he might have seen a few crime scenes in his day.

"I understand you want to talk to me. What is it you want?"

"I'll get right to the point. I would like to see who you have under the sheet. A friend of mine is missing. I simply want to make sure that it isn't him."

"How long has this friend of yours been missing?"

"A few hours. We believe that he is in danger and that he came to this lighthouse with a woman. I have not seen either of them."

"And what is your name?"

"My name is Nick McCord. I am a. . ."

"I know who you are," he said interrupting me. "Your reputation as an expert on preserving crime scenes proceeds you. I've read your manual on "Preserving the Crime Scene". I'm Detective John Swain."

"It's nice to meet someone who has actually read it," I replied as I took his outstretched hand and shook it.

I glanced over his shoulder and saw the rookie cop standing behind Detective Swain. The expression on his face was priceless.

"What is it that I can do for you?"

"I know that you are busy right now, but I would consider it a very big favor if you could tell me who it is under that sheet?"

"We don't know, yet. You want to take a look?"

"Sure, if it doesn't interfere with your investigation."

"No problem. We just got here. We don't even know what happened, yet," he said as we walked toward the body.

I stood and looked down at the white sheet spread over the body. I was reluctant to look for fear that it was Tom under that sheet, but it had to be done. I had to know.

I knelt down and carefully lifted up the corner of the sheet. There was the body of a man lying on the hard path all twisted in ways that were not normal. It was clear that he had struck the ground after a long fall, striking the edge of the hard pathway. He looked as if the fall had broken almost every bone in his body.

I let out a long sigh of relief to discover that the body was not Tom. There was no hiding my relief. I turned my head and looked up at Detective Swain. I shook my head to indicate that it was not who I was looking for.

I looked up to see where the man had fallen from. There was a metal rail that seemed to be pushed out away from the bricks around the tower of the lighthouse.

"You have any idea who this man is?" Detective Swain asked.

"I don't think I've ever seen him before," I replied as I stood up. "Have you been up there, where he fell from?"

"Not yet. Like I said, we just got here. I was about to go up. Would you care to join me?"

"No, I don't think so. Take a good look at where the iron rail is hooked to the building. It looks like the supports of the rail were embedded in the mortar of the bricks. You might find that it was an accident," I suggested.

Detective Swain looked up at the place where the iron rail was loose, then back at me.

"You might be right."

I took a moment to look around where the body lay.

"Look here," I said as I pointed to several small pieces of red brick and pieces of mortar that lay on the pathway and in the grass at the edge of the pathway.

"Yeah, I see them."

"I'd almost be willing to bet that he was leaning out over the rail too far. My guess would be that the rail gave way from his weight and he simply fell."

"I'll check it out. And as your manual says, don't take anything for granted," he said with a smile.

"That's right."

Just then the crime scene investigators arrived. Detective Swain gave them a quick review of the scene and turned it over to them. If they determined that a crime had been committed, they would gather all the evidence and turn the case back over to the detective to follow up on. Until then, there was little that Detective Swain could do but wait for them to finish their work. He already had officers interviewing witnesses.

"What brings you to Marquette?" he asked as he walked along side me while I walked toward Monica.

"I'm here on vacation. My fiancée and I are on a cruise of the Great Lakes. We are going to get married on the ship."

"Well, congratulations."

"Thank you," I replied. "By the way, this is my fiancée, Doctor Monica Barnhart. Monica, this is Detective John Swain."

"Nice to meet you, Detective," Monica said.

"Nice to meet you, too. I wish it could be under different circumstances," he said politely.

"It wasn't Tom," I said to Monica.

I could see the look of relief in her eyes. When I glanced over at Detective Swain, I got the feeling he wanted to know about our missing friend and why I thought he was in danger.

"I'm sure you would like to know what's going on and why I thought the body under that sheet might have been my friend. If you have a minute or two, I'll explain."

"I would appreciate that," he replied as I pointed to the bench and gestured for him to sit down. As soon as he sat down, I sat down next to Monica.

I began by explaining that I no longer worked for the Milwaukee Police Department and that I was a private investigator now. I also told him about the case I had been dragged into by the Captain of the cruise liner. As I explained about Tom and Thorndike, Detective Swain seemed to grasp the reason for my concern.

"Is there anything that I can do? You understand that I can't get directly involved as this is out of my jurisdiction. My boss would be on my ass. Oh, excuse me," he said to Monica. "I would be in deep trouble with my boss."

"I understand. I don't want to get you in any trouble. The Coast Guard and the state police are doing what they can, but it has proven to be slow. The only thing that concerns me at the moment is finding Tom and Pamela."

"Why don't you give me their full names and a description of them, and I'll see what I can do to find them."

"I'd appreciate that."

"If we find them before you, where can I get in touch with you?" Detective Swain asked.

"You can call the ship and leave a message with Captain Klausen. I've been working with him."

"You call me if you find them first," he said as he gave me one of his business cards.

After I gave him their full names and a description of each of them, he stood up and bid us goodbye. He went over to his car to broadcast the descriptions of Tom and Pamela over the police radio.

We left the lighthouse and headed back to the ship by cab. All the way back, we looked up and down the streets in the hope of finding them. When we arrived at the ship, we checked with the ship's officer on duty at the gangplank. He told us that Tom and Pamela had returned to the ship almost an hour ago. He also informed me that Higgins had not returned to the ship yet.

"Let the Captain know as soon as Higgins returns. I want to know as well. If he doesn't return by the time the ship is ready to sail, I need to know that immediately. And don't say anything to Higgins. Do you understand?"

"Yes, sir."

"If you have any questions, contact your Captain."

"Yes, sir. Captain Klausen has instructed us to cooperate with you in any way that we can, sir," the duty officer assured me.

"Thank you."

Monica and I went directly to Pamela's cabin. I looked at Monica as I hesitated to knock on the door. If they had been back for almost an hour, they could be doing something that they would rather we didn't disturb.

"Are you going to knock or not," Monica asked.

I shrugged my shoulders, reached over and knocked on the door. As I waited for a response, I could hear nothing from inside the cabin. I had been hoping that they would be there. I had no idea how Pamela would react to the news that she might be one of the targets of a murderer. It would make it so much easier to sit down and explain what we thought we knew in the privacy of her cabin. It would give them a chance to let it soak in before they had to go out in public again. Not everyone can accept the news that someone out there wants them dead in a calm and cool manner.

When I didn't get an answer, I knocked again. I still didn't get an answer.

"Where do you think they might be?" I asked, as I looked at my watch.

"Do you think they might be in the lounge? It's not really time for dinner," Monica asked.

"Could be," I replied.

I took Monica by the arm and we headed for the lounge.

* * * *

As we walked into the lounge, we looked around for Tom and Pamela. I was the first to spot them. They were sitting in a booth holding hands.

"There they are," I said as I gently took Monica's arm and started to guide her in their direction.

"Hi," Pamela said with a smile.

"Hi. We've been looking for you guys. Where have you been?" Monica asked as we slipped into the booth across from them.

"We went on the tour of "Anatomy of A Murder". It was very interesting," Tom said.

"Did you go any place else?" I asked.

"We went through a few of the local shops. We thought about going out to the lighthouse, but decided against it. We took a riding tour of the historic district instead," Pamela said.

"What did you guys do?" Tom asked.

"We went looking for the two of you," Monica said.

"Why? We thought that you guys were going on the lighthouse tour," Pamela said.

"We were, but something came up. I think we should go back to our suite. We have something to talk to you about, and I don't think this is the place to talk about it," I said.

The tone of my voice and the look on my face must have given them some idea of how serious what I had to say was to them. There was also no doubt in my mind that it was important for them to hear everything I had to say. I watched as Pamela and Tom looked at each other, then they looked at us.

"I assure you, this is important," Monica said slowly and clearly so there would be no misunderstanding.

"Okay," Tom replied, and then looked at Pamela.

Tom nodded for Pamela to slide out of the booth. As she did, Monica slid out of the booth on our side. We all walked back to our suite without a word and went inside.

"I don't mind saying so, but the two of you have me a little scared," Pamela said as I closed the door.

"I'm sorry about that, I really am, but what we have to talk to you about will probably justify your feelings," I said.

Pamela looked at me as if she thought that I might be crazy. I wasn't sure but that she might be right. Either way, I felt that we could not keep what we suspected from them. They needed to know that their lives might be in danger. To keep that information from them would make it harder to protect them. I didn't want them going around thinking that there was nothing to worry about when they had everything to worry about.

They sat down on the loveseat while I took a minute to call Detective Swain to let him know that we had found them. He seemed relieved, and I thanked him for his concern.

As soon as I hung up, I sat down next to Monica. We began by telling them what we knew, and what we thought we knew, about the murders and Mr. Higgins. I could see that Tom was listening very carefully. When we got to the part about thinking that Higgins was really Thorndike, I thought I could see Tom start to try to mentally put things together.

On the other hand, I think what we were telling them added to Pamela's fears. Her eyes were big, and she kept looking from me to Tom to Monica and back to me. It was probably a little too much for her to comprehend, let alone understand with any degree of reality. After all, this was probably the first time that she had been exposed to this much violence and death in such a short time. Plus there was the fact that it was all happening on a cruise ship which left her with no way to leave it behind.

Pamela knew a little about the lodge and the stash of treasure that had been there. Tom had told her about that, at least most of it. She was still having a hard time dealing with the fact that two people had been murdered on the same ship she was on. Now we were telling her that she might become a victim, too.

"What do you think, Tom? Do you think that Higgins could be Thorndike?" I asked.

It was clear that Tom was thinking hard about Higgins and that he was trying to remember some of the traits that Thorndike had displayed at the lodge. It was not an easy thing to do for anyone. Tom had to bring up past memories that I was sure he would rather forget.

"Damn Nick, I just don't know," Tom said, his face showing his frustration. "I will admit that what you have told us put things in a different light."

"What do you mean?"

"I'll never look at Higgins the same again," he replied.

"I don't suppose you will, but that's the point. I don't want you to look at him in the same way. I need you to compare him to what you can remember about Thorndike. What I need to know is do you think that Higgins is Thorndike or not?"

"And if he is, what then?" Tom asked.

"I can have him arrested immediately and returned to prison. You have to remember that he is wanted for escaping from a prison. That alone will keep him jailed until we can sort out the rest," I replied.

"And if he escapes again? What then?" Pamela asked sharply.

"I doubt that he will escape again. He was already serving a life sentence for murder. His escape will put him in a higher security part of the prison where he will not be able to be with anyone.".

"I can't be sure. What is it you want me to do?" Tom asked.

"I want you to watch Higgins and see if you think he is really Thorndike."

"You're asking Tom to stick his neck out to prove something that you already know? That's absurd," Pamela said with a note of disgust, along with a tone of anger, in her voice.

"We have to know for sure," Monica said calmly.

"I can't believe that you could go along with this," Pamela said to Monica.

"And you," Pamela said to me, "How can you ask your best friend to stick his neck out like this. What kind of a friend are you?" she demanded.

"The kind that would do whatever it takes to keep his friend from becoming the third dead body on this ship," I replied sharply.

As soon as I said it I was sorry. I had said what I did not so much in anger as from the frustration I was feeling at the moment. She was afraid for Tom and I couldn't blame her for that. I was afraid for him, too. She was in love with him and that tends to change the way a person looks at things.

I had known Tom for a very long time, much longer than she had. She didn't seem to understand that I would do anything for him. The last thing I wanted was for Tom to get injured or killed.

"Nick, Pamela, this is getting us nowhere. We have a problem here," Monica said.

"Monica's right. Nick is just trying to keep us safe," Tom said to Pamela as he reached out and took hold of her hand.

"I'm sorry, Pamela. I don't mean to make it sound like I don't care what happens to anyone as long as I get the killer. I don't want to stick anyone out there to become the killer's next victim. I won't do that. The one thing you have to understand is that Tom, and you because you are with him, are already out there. You're already targets. If Higgins is Thorndike, and he suspects that Tom might recognize him, then Tom is already in danger. The fact that you are with him puts you in the same danger," I tried to explain.

"You see, Pamela, Nick is truly Tom's best friend. He is not trying to put Tom in danger, or you for that matter. He is trying to protect both of you, and that's not easy," Monica said softly.

"There are only two ways he can do that. One is to hide you in a cabin with guards at the door for the rest of the trip, or until the danger is no longer there. Or he can have Tom identify Thorndike and get him arrested before he kills anyone else," Monica explained.

Pamela looked at Monica as she listened to her. I couldn't say for sure, but I think Monica's gentle explanation and the soft tones of her voice helped Pamela to see the logic in what we were trying to do.

She looked over at Tom. Slowly, the expression on her face changed to one that showed she was beginning to understand and could see the logic in it.

"Honey, we need to do this," Tom said softly.

"Okay," she conceded somewhat reluctantly. "I don't like it; but if it's what has to be done, then I guess we need to do it."

Tom smiled at her, then leaned over and kissed her lightly on the cheek. He then turned and looked at me.

"What do you want me to do?"

"We are going to dinner in a little while. I want you to watch Higgins's every move and see if you can positively identify him as Thorndike. If you can, we can have him arrested immediately and that will end the threat on your life," I explained.

"I'll try," he agreed.

"You have to be sure. Don't read anything into what he does. Simply watch him and compare what he does to what you can remember about Thorndike. If he does things in the same way, we have him," I explained to Tom.

We sat around our suite for a little while in order to get nerves settled before we all went to dinner. I was hoping that Higgins would show up in the dining room for dinner so Tom would have the opportunity to observe him.

CHAPTER SEVENTEEN

When it was time for dinner the four of us left our suite and started for the dining room. I was a bit worried about moving around in the passageways. It would be a very difficult place to protect Tom and Pamela. The passageways were narrow and there were a lot of corners making it easy for someone to attack us and disappear quickly.

I stayed alert for any possibility of running into Higgins while we were going to the restaurant. The last thing I wanted was for harm to come to any of us.

We got to the restaurant without incident. As luck would have it, Higgins was not there. I was pleased that we arrived before Higgins. It gave me time to get set so that Tom could observe Higgins without making it too obvious what we were doing.

I requested a table that would give as many of us as possible a good view of the room. When we were shown to a table, I dismissed the waiter and seated everyone where I wanted them.

I had Tom sit down with his back to the wall so he could see anyone who came into the room. He would be able to see Higgins no matter where he chose to sit. I had Monica sit across the table from where I was going to sit.

Pamela was the only one with her back to the room. I got the impression from the look on her face that she didn't like it much, but I felt that was a good position for her as she was having difficulty controlling her fears. The last thing I wanted was for her to tip our hand before we were ready. I couldn't help but feel that there was a chance that she might panic if she saw Higgins, or if he came close to us.

If she panicked, there was no telling what Higgins might do. He could, of course, do nothing, which is what I would expect if I was wrong and he wasn't Thorndike. But if I was right, he could erupt into violence and kill or injure some innocent bystanders. I couldn't take that chance.

I sat down beside Tom, which gave me a pretty good view of most of the dining room. There was only a small area of the room that was difficult for me to see without turning almost my whole body around, and Monica was in a position to watch that for me. All I could do from this point on was watch what happened and do the best I could to protect Tom and the others from harm.

"You all right with this," I asked Tom in a whisper.

"I'm not," Pamela said with a bit of anger in her voice before Tom could respond to me.

"Pamela, Honey, we have to do this. If we don't, we will have no idea if Higgins is really Thorndike or not," he said trying to make her understand.

"I still don't like it."

"Listen, if this is too much for you, I can have you escorted back to your cabin and have a guard posted outside your door twenty-four hours a day until this is over. Is that what you want?" I said looking her right in the eyes.

I wasn't really happy about it myself. And I certainly didn't need Pamela's fears getting in the way. Besides, we had been through all of it in our suite. We didn't need to go over it again in the dining room. I didn't need someone sitting there who might screw up the whole thing and possibly get someone hurt.

"No, of course not, but you don't even know if the man that was killed across the ship from us was mistaken for Tom or not."

"That's true, I don't know for sure. But there is a better than even chance that he was. That is one of the things we are trying to find out. If he was mistaken for Tom, then you are in as much danger as Tom. If he wasn't, then you and Tom will be able to go about your business without fear of someone trying to kill you in the middle of the night. Which is what you want, isn't it?"

We sat at the table and looked at Pamela while we waited for an answer from her. She may have been a very beautiful woman, but I was beginning to wonder if she wasn't letting her emotions run her life. The thought also passed through my mind that I was being too hard on her. She had probably led a pretty sheltered life.

"I'm sorry if I sound a little callus about all this, but like it or not, I know what it takes to stop someone like Thorndike," I said.

I watched her as she looked at me, then slowly tipped her head down and looked at the table directly in front of her. She then looked up at Tom. Her eyes seemed to be pleading for him to understand how she felt.

"It's okay, Honey. I understand how you feel, but we must do as Nick says if we are going to have the freedom to do as we please," Tom said to her as he reached out across the table and took hold of her hand.

I noticed a slight smile come over Pamela's face. I also noticed that she squeezed his hand. Maybe now she would settle down and be ready for whatever happened.

I glanced at Monica, and then took a quick look around the room, as much of it as I could see. When I looked back at Monica, she shook her head slightly to indicate that she had not seen Higgins.

The waiter came over and took our order. It didn't seem that any of us were very hungry. The evening dragged on at a snail's pace. We all took our time eating. After dinner we ordered after dinner drinks and sat around waiting. It didn't look as if we were going to see Higgins tonight. It was beginning to look like this was all for nothing.

We talked, but it was about little unimportant things. I was about to say something to Tom when I noticed one of the ship's officers coming across the room toward me.

182

"Mr. McCord, the Captain wants you to know that we are about to shove off for Thunder Bay. He also wanted you to know that Mr. Higgins, Oliver Higgins, has just come back aboard the ship with his wife."

"Can you confirm if the woman he returned with is the same woman he left with?"

"Yes, sir. It is the same woman."

"Thank you," I said as I began to think.

I had to wonder if I had made a mistake. There was a possibility that I might have selected the wrong Mr. Higgins.

"What's the matter, Nick?" Monica asked.

"I was so sure that it was Oliver Higgins that was Thorndike, but now I'm not so sure."

"What makes you think that it isn't Oliver Higgins?"

"He left with a woman that has been described as his wife. And he returned from shore with that same woman. Does that sound like Thorndike to you?"

"Not really, but it could be. Have you looked at some of the passengers on this ship?" Monica asked.

"No, not really," I replied wondering what she was getting at.

"There are a lot of older women on the ship. I'd be willing to bet that a number of them are widowed or have never married," Monica said.

I thought about what she was saying and remembered that I had seen a number of women traveling alone, simply cruising around the Great Lakes enjoying the tour. Monica might be right. There was a very good chance that my first thought was correct.

Thorndike could have easily picked out a woman that was going ashore and walked down the gangplank with her. It would have been just as easy for him to wait for her to return to the ship and walk back up the gangplank with her. There was also the possibility that he had spent the entire day with her to make them look like any other couple enjoying a cruise. It would make a good cover for him. There was no question that he would have plenty of witnesses.

There was also the fact that Harvey Higgins was much younger. He would have been closer to Thorndike's age, but he was a smaller man than Thorndike. It would be hard for a man of Thorndike's height to disguise himself as a smaller person.

There was also the fact that the older Higgins only looked older. It would be easy for Thorndike to make himself look older. The fact that I couldn't get it out of my mind that he didn't walk like the old man he appeared to be only helped to convince me that the older Higgins was really Thorndike.

As I thought about everything that we knew and the things that we thought we knew, I stared at the drink on the table in front of me. The ice had caused water to condense on the outside of the glass. As I picked up the glass, I could see the ring made on the cocktail napkin it had been setting on.

As I started to tip up the glass and take a drink, my eyes were drawn to Monica across the table. There was a strange look on her face. She was not looking at me. She appeared to be looking past me at something behind me.

I set the glass back down and glanced over at Tom. I noticed that he was watching something behind me, too. It would have been more accurate to say that he was studying someone behind me.

When I looked back at Monica, she was now looking at me. She nodded her head slightly. I was sure that she was trying to tell me that Higgins was in the room, and that he was sitting behind me. I quickly looked over at Tom again.

"That's him," Tom whispered, and then he turned and looked at me. "That's him."

"Are you sure?" I asked softly, needing to know for sure that it really was Thorndike.

"Yes. There's no doubt in my mind. That's Thorndike."

"What do we do now?" Monica asked quietly as she looked at me.

"There are a lot of people in here. We can't confront him now without risking someone getting hurt."

"Then what do we do?" Pamela asked, the tone of her voice showing me that she was scared.

"We wait," I replied calmly.

I was reluctant to wait long, as I was not sure if Pamela and Tom could keep their cool for very long. It was important that he not suspect that we were watching him. If he became aware of us watching him and got too nervous, things could erupt in nothing flat. If that happened, who knows who might get hurt. I couldn't risk that happening, not here.

On the other hand, it was important that we get him out of circulation as soon as possible, before he killed someone else. I knew that he was the type of person who didn't care who got hurt as long as his goals were met.

I looked around the room as much as I could without turning around so Thorndike could catch me looking his way. I was hoping that there was a ship's officer hanging around. I needed to get word to the Captain that we had found Thorndike in the dining room. If I could do that, the Captain might be able to send some help before things got out of hand and turned ugly.

I noticed a waiter standing off to the side. He was leaning against the wall next to the door. His hands were folded in front of him as he looked around the room. He looked as if he was waiting for someone to request something.

As casually as possible, I motioned for the waiter to come to our table. As soon as I caught his eye, he smiled slightly and started walking toward our table.

"What are you doing?" Monica asked.

"I'm going to try to get the waiter to get the Captain and a few of his men," I replied.

"What if Thorndike sees the waiter go out of the dining room?"

"I don't know, but I can't think of anything else at the moment. It's a chance we'll have to take."

Monica nodded her head that she agreed with my assessment of the situation. I'm sure she also knew that our situation was very volatile. One mistake and anything could happen.

"May I help you, sir," the waiter said with a smile.

"Write this down," I said quietly and slowly. "Thorndike in dining room. Need help to capture."

The waiter looked at me as if I were crazy. But when I nodded at his order pad, he began to write.

"Get that message to your captain. But leave the dining room as if you are going to get a bottle of your best wine. Do you understand?" I asked softly.

"Yes, sir," the waiter replied nervously.

I casually waved the waiter away and watched him as he left the dining room. He looked a little excited and nervous. I could only hope that Higgins didn't notice. I wished that the waiter could have been a bit more casual about his departure, but what was done was done and there was nothing I could do about it.

"I sure hope it doesn't take the Captain too long to get here. If he leaves, we could have a problem."

"Don't look now, but I think he's leaving," Monica said.

I closed my eyes and almost prayed that he would sit back down, but he didn't.

"What's he doing?" I asked Monica.

"He's putting a tip on the table. He glanced over here. Now he's headed for the door."

I was able to see him at that point. I watched him as he walked out of the dining room. At the last minute, he turned and glanced back over his shoulder at me. There was no doubt in my mind that he knew we had been watching him. There was also no doubt in my mind that he knew we had figured out who he was.

"Stay here. I don't want any of you leaving this room until the Captain gets here," I said as I stood up.

"Where are you going?" Monica asked.

"I need to know where he's going."

* * * *

I quickly headed for the door of the dining room. When I got to it, I stopped and looked out into the passageway in time to see Thorndike disappear around the corner to one of the stairwells.

When I reached the corner, I looked up and down the stairwell but didn't see him. I thought I heard someone going down, so I followed. The stairwell led down to Deck Two. I wasn't sure what was on Deck Two except for cabins. I had only been on that deck to leave the ship and to investigate the first murder. I hadn't paid any attention to anything else.

Suddenly it occurred to me that I had no idea where Thorndike's cabin was located. There was a good chance that he was headed for it.

As I stepped onto Deck Two from the stairwell, I hesitated at the corner and peered around it. I looked down the passageway, but saw no one. I listened carefully in the hope of hearing a door close or footsteps on the stairwell leading down to Deck One. I heard nothing, not a sound.

I began to wonder where he went. Since there was no one in the passageway, I began to think that he might have gone on down another level. With nothing else to go on but gut feeling, I decided to go down one more level. If I found him, all the better. If I didn't, I would quickly return to the dining room.

I took another quick look down the hall, and then took a deep breath. I turned and looked down the stairwell to the deck below. Something in my mind told me that I shouldn't go down there until I had some backup from the Captain, but finding him was important.

I turned and started down the steps to the deck below. Before looking around the corner I took a moment to listen in the hope of hearing something, some noise that would tell me where he went. I heard nothing, nothing at all.

As I started to step around the corner, I thought I heard something behind me. I started to turn around when I suddenly saw something coming at me out of the corner of my eye. I felt a sharp blow to the side of my head as I tried to duck, but it was too late. Stars appeared in my eyes, and then everything went black.

CHAPTER EIGHTEEN

I could hear the sounds of footsteps running down the passageway and voices. Although the footsteps seemed to be fading away in one direction, the voices seemed to be coming closer from the other. Then I heard the sound of someone running toward me. There was a dull throbbing pain on the side of my head as I began to remember what had happened before the lights went out.

"Are you all right," a male voice said.

I opened my eyes and looked up to see two men and two women standing over me. They were in evening attire and looked as if they were either coming from the lounge or going to the lounge for an evening of dancing.

"Sam, go call for help," one man said as he looked at the other man.

"No. I'll be all right once I get to my feet," I said, but I wasn't all that sure it would be that easy.

"Are you sure? It looks like you took a pretty nasty hit on the side of the head," the man said as he reached down to help me up.

"I'll be fine. It'll just take me a minute to get my balance."

I had to admit that I felt a little woozy for a minute or so when I first stood up. However, my head seemed to clear quickly. The side of my head hurt some, but it didn't hurt as much as the feeling of stupidity that I felt for walking into a trap like some rookie cop.

Once the dizziness cleared, I reached up and touched the side of my head. It stung so I knew that I had an open wound. I had blood on my fingers. It was not much blood, for which I was thankful.

I began to realize that I had not been out for more than a few seconds. It was also clear that if it hadn't been for the four people who came down the passageway when they did, Thorndike might have had time to kill me.

"I would like to thank you for coming to my aid," I said.

"We're just glad that you are going to be all right. I think you should get that cut looked after by the ship's doctor," the one man said.

"Yes, and I think you should report this to the captain as soon as possible," one of the ladies said.

"Thank you, I will," I assured her.

"It's dreadful what has happened on this ship. I have never been on a cruise that has had so many problems," the older of the ladies said in disgust.

"I'm sure you're right, Ma'am. I'll talk to the captain about it. Again, thank you," I said then started down the passageway toward the stairwell.

I checked my watch. I had only been gone from the dining room for a few minutes, but it was long enough for Monica to be worried. I needed to find her and let her know that I was okay.

When I got back to our suite, I found that Monica was not there. I figured that she was still in the dining room. As I turned to leave our suite and go to the dining room, I caught sight of my reflection in the mirror. I had blood on the side of my face and on my shirt. I didn't think it would set well if I returned to the dining room all bloody.

I sat down on the edge of the bed, picked up the phone and placed a call to the dining room. I asked for Monica. While I waited for her to come to the phone, I tried to decide what I was going to say to her that would not cause her to get too excited.

"Hello?"

"Monica, this is Nick."

"Where are you?"

"I'm in our suite."

"What are you doing there?"

"Listen, is the Captain with you?"

"Yes, he is. He just got here."

"I want you to bring him to our suite. I want you to have Tom and Pamela go to her cabin and wait for us. Do you understand?" I asked.

"Yes. What's going on?"

"Did the Captain bring anyone with him?"

"Yes. He brought two of his crew."

"Ask him to have them stand guard outside Pamela's door until we have had a chance to talk."

"Okay. Nick, are you hurt?" Monica asked.

"Yes, but it's nothing serious."

"I'll be there in a minute," Monica said without any hesitation.

"Monica, make sure that Tom and Pamela get to her cabin safely. Thorndike knows we are on to him."

"Okay," she replied, then hung up.

While I waited for Monica to return, I went into the bathroom and took off my shirt. I checked the cut on the side of my head. The cut was not very deep and had stopped bleeding.

I washed the blood off my face and the side of my head. I checked the wound again to make sure it wasn't bleeding. It looked pretty clean, and I didn't think it would require any stitches. I put a bandage over the cut and found a clean shirt.

I was putting on the clean shirt when I heard the door to our suite open. I turned as Monica and Captain Klausen came into the suite.

"Are you okay?" Monica asked as she hurried across the room to me.

"I'm fine. It's nothing serious. Did you get Tom and Pamela to her cabin?"

"Yes, we did," Captain Klausen replied.

"Good. I want you to keep a guard on them until we find Thorndike and get him locked up."

"What happened to you?"

"I ran into Thorndike. He took off."

"So I take it you have figured out who this Thorndike is posing as?"

"Yes, sir. He is posing as Oliver Higgins."

"Oliver Higgins has a wife and is quite old," Captain Klausen said, the expression on his face showing that he wasn't so sure that I was right.

"The woman that Oliver Higgins was seen with is not his wife. I believe that she is just a lonely passenger that he has attached himself to in order to make it look like he is with his wife."

"Are you sure?" he asked.

"I wasn't at first, but I have no doubt about it now," I replied.

It took me a few minutes to explain it. There was little doubt in my mind that Captain Klausen understood, and that he was able to piece the puzzle together as well as we had. After all, he had seen all the reports, too. There was also the fact that he had been involved in the investigation to some degree from the very first night.

"What do you think we should do now?" he asked.

"It's your ship, sir. You have the last word," I replied.

"I have been given instructions to cooperate with you in any way I can. This is an area where you are far more qualified to proceed than I. I will certainly bow to your expertise," he said looking to me for direction.

"In that case, sir, I want you to keep guards on Pamela's cabin and keep both Tom and Pamela in the cabin until we find and capture Thorndike."

"I have two armed men standing outside her cabin right now. What next?"

"We have to find Thorndike."

"Where did you see him last?" Captain Klausen asked.

"On Deck One."

"Deck One? What was he doing on Deck One? There aren't that many cabins on that deck."

"My best guess would be that he was suckering me down there. If it hadn't been for some folks going from their cabins to the lounge for the evening, I might not be here to tell you about it."

"Oliver Higgins' cabin in located on Deck Two," Captain Klausen stated.

"Isn't that the same deck where Lancaster was murdered?" I asked.

"Yes. Higgins' cabin is half way down the passageway and on the other side of the ship. His cabin number is two-sixty-six."

"That is interesting. It would have taken Thorndike only a few minutes to get back to his cabin after killing Lancaster," I said as I thought about it.

"That's about right."

"And late at night, there was very little chance that he would have been seen. Guests on the ship were pretty tired after the first day out in the wind and sun."

"That's probably true, also," the Captain agreed.

"It would have been easy for him to remove any of the stolen loot from Lancaster's cabin without being seen. He probably could have made several trips without being seen if he was careful," I said thoughtfully.

"That's probably true, too."

"The only thing that still puzzles me is what went wrong?"

"I don't understand," Captain Klausen asked.

"Something went wrong after they got aboard the ship and it had set sail."

"What makes you think that?"

"The killing of Lancaster was very messy. That would indicate that it was not well planned out. That means that something went wrong after they were aboard the ship."

"I see," Captain Klausen agreed by nodding his head.

"We could use a couple of armed men. I want to go to Thorndike's room."

"I'll get them down here. Do you have a gun, Mr. McCord?"

"No."

"I'll have them bring one for you."

Captain Klausen went to the phone and placed a call to the bridge. I couldn't hear what he was saying, but he was giving someone clear and concise instructions.

"We will have backup and weapons in a few minutes. I also checked to make sure that we had the right cabin number for Oliver Higgins' cabin. I would surely hate to go charging into the wrong cabin."

"So would I," I replied.

* * * *

It didn't take long before there was a knock on our cabin door. Captain Klausen got up and walked over to the door. He peered through the peephole, then reached down and opened the door.

Standing outside our cabin were two well armed crewmembers. One of them had a small metal box tucked under his arm. Captain Klausen stepped back and let them into our suite. As the first crewmen stepped inside, he handed the small box to the Captain, then stepped back and waited for instructions.

I watched as Captain Klausen took a key from his pocket and opened the box. He drew out two pistols from the box and handed one to me.

"I hope we don't need these," he said.

"I can assure you that we will. Thorndike will not give up very easily. He is probably well armed himself."

The expression on Captain Klausen's face was one that told me that he was hoping that I was wrong, but he knew that I was more than likely right. For the first time, I think he got the message that it was not going to be a simple cuff and stuff arrest. I already knew that. I had the misfortune of having dealt with Thorndike and many others like him before. Something I was sure the Captain had not experienced, yet.

"I hope that no one gets hurt," the Captain said.

"So do I, but you have to remember, Thorndike is like a trapped animal. There is nowhere for him to go until we get to Thunder Bay.

"He can't jump over the side and swim to safety. First of all, I doubt that he is that good a swimmer. Secondly, the water in Lake Superior is very cold and will kill him in short order. He might last for about fifteen minutes without a wet suit. If he has a wet suit, he will last maybe a couple of hours, if he's darn lucky. You can count on the fact that he knows full well that he is trapped aboard the ship."

"That means he's somewhere on the ship," the Captain said.

"That's right, and we have no idea where. We will find him even if we have to search every single inch of it."

"Then we best get started," the Captain said.

"We'll start with his room. There may be a clue as to what he has in mind. I can't believe that he would come aboard a ship without having some kind of a plan should he be discovered," I said.

"Right," the Captain agreed.

I turned to Monica.

"I want you to stay in Pamela's room with her and Tom. There will be guards on the door."

"Okay," she replied, giving no sign that she objected to being left behind this time.

We opened the cabin door and looked out into the hall. The hall was clear except for the two armed guards standing in front of Pamela's door. I quickly escorted Monica to Pamela's cabin and went inside with her.

I took a minute to explain to Pamela and Tom what was going on. I also explained what I wanted them to do, which was to stay in the cabin until the Captain or I told them it was safe.

Tom offered to help in the search for Thorndike, but I didn't think that was a good idea. Tom had no experience with a gun, and I certainly didn't want him running around the ship looking for Thorndike without one.

When I was about to leave the cabin, I heard Captain Klausen give clear instructions to the guards that they were not to leave the cabin unguarded for even a second. The hour was late and the ship was well on its way. It appeared that a day of touring the town had caused most of the passengers to turn in as the ship's passageways were quiet.

After all were set, the Captain led the search party down the passageways and stairwells to Deck Two. When we arrived on Deck Two, the Captain stopped to make sure that everyone was ready.

"You," the Captain said as he pointed at one of the armed crewmen. "I want you to go around and come up on the other end of the passageway and make sure that no one comes down the back stairwell. We don't need any innocent passengers getting in the way and possibly getting hurt."

"Yes, sir," the crewmen said.

Without another word, the crewmen took off at a dead run around the corner. It was just a minute or two before he showed up at the other end of the passageway. He got into position then signaled that he was ready.

After we checked our guns, I led the Captain and the other crewmen slowly down the passageway. We stayed very close to the wall because there was little cover for any of us if Thorndike came charging out of his cabin with his gun blazing. We had no idea if he actually had a gun, but I would have bet that he did.

When I was only a few feet from the door to cabin two-sixty-six, I stopped and put my head against the wall. I could not hear any sounds at all. I glanced back to see Captain Klausen standing directly behind me, his gun held tightly in his hand. I was almost sure that the palms of his hands were sweating. There were little beads of sweat on his forehead. The young crewman behind him looked like he was scared, too.

I could hardly blame them. This was not the ideal situation to be in. As far as we knew, we had an armed criminal who had nothing to look forward to except the death penalty if he was caught.

On the other hand, the rest of us had our lives and families to think about. He clearly had the advantage even though he was outnumbered. I knew from experience that criminals that have nothing to lose often do strange things. Things that a normal person would never consider doing.

It was time, time to open the door and find out if he was inside. To knock first would leave it open for a gun battle. The last thing I wanted was a gun battle in the passageway of a cruise ship.

I motioned for the Captain to give me the key to the cabin. I waited until he found the key and handed it to me. Since I was on the wrong side of the door, I quietly slipped past the door to the other side and leaned up against the wall.

I took a deep breath before I looked down at the keyhole in the lock. After making sure that I had the key right side up, I carefully slipped the key into the lock. I did everything I could to make sure that I made as little noise as possible.

Once the key was in the door, I looked up at the Captain. I wanted everyone ready when I turned the key and pushed the door open.

I got into position to bust through the door. After taking a deep breath and glancing over to see if everyone was ready, I quickly turned the key and shoved hard against the door. The door flew open and we all rushed in with guns at the ready.

CHAPTER NINETEEN

The four of us charged through the door expecting a violent confrontation with Thorndike. There was no doubt in my mind that he would do whatever it took to prevent us from capturing him. After all, he had nothing to lose by killing another person. We were just as determined to prevent him from harming anyone, including us.

However, a quick check of the cabin, including the closet and the bathroom revealed that there was no one there. I looked at the Captain. The expression on his face was that of surprise. He had expected to find Thorndike in the cabin, too.

"Stand at ease," the Captain said to his men.

I watched as the two crewmen put their guns back in their holsters and stood by to wait for instructions.

"Any ideas as to where he might be?" I asked the Captain.

"No," he replied.

Captain Klausen seemed as confused at I was. We both knew that there had to be hundreds of places to hide on the ship.

I began to look the cabin over from where I was standing. The first thing I noticed was the in-cabin safe. It seemed that it might have been emptied in a hurry, as the door was standing wide open.

Wherever Thorndike had gone, he had taken the stolen jewelry with him. The question was where had he gone?

"Captain, have your men watch the passageway. I'm going to take a look around.

The captain turned to his men to see if they had heard me. They acknowledged my instructions by nodding to the Captain that they understood. The Captain nodded and they quickly turned around and went to the door to wait and watch.

I stood in one spot for a minute or two looking around. I had seen nothing that was of interest to me except for the fact that the place looked as if the occupant would be returning at any time.

I stepped up to the dresser and pulled open the top drawer. There were several pairs of underwear and socks neatly folded and stacked in the drawer. A quick search of the drawer produced nothing else. In the second drawer were several shirts and other clothing, also neatly folded. A search of that drawer produced nothing. I found the bottom drawer to be completely empty.

I went over to the closet and opened it. I found several sets of shirts and pants hung neatly on the rack. The clothes were typical of those that I had seen Oliver Higgins wear. There were also several pairs of shoes lined up on the floor.

As I pushed back some of the clothes in order to see what might be in back of the closet, I found a makeup kit. It was a large one similar to the kind used by actors. It opened on the top and had several drawers in it.

I pulled the makeup kit out of the closet and set it on the desk. I opened the top and discovered two men's wigs. They were gray with a few strains of black running through them and were combed in the same style as Oliver Higgins combed his hair. There were also some fake bushy eyebrows, like Oliver Higgins had. I turned and looked at the Captain as he leaned against the door waiting for me to complete my search of the cabin.

"I think we've found Oliver Higgins," I said as I held up one of the wigs for the Captain to see.

"It would appear so," he replied. "Are we now looking for this Thorndike fella?"

"It appears that we might be. I don't know how many wigs he had. He may look completely different by now.

There's no telling how many disguises he could make from what's in this kit."

"The one thing we do know is that he doesn't have the makeup kit any more. He can't change his appearance that much without it," the Captain pointed out.

"Maybe, maybe not," I said.

Another look around the room seemed to confirm my suspicion that he had cleared out in a hurry. The more I thought about it, the more I realized that he had almost been seen in the passageway when he attacked me. He probably knew that he had not killed me and that as soon as I was able I would go after him again. That left him with few choices.

"Our Mr. Andrew Thorndike is now on the run. He's got to know that I know who he is and that I will be looking for him. Even a complete idiot would know that he would not be safe here. Where could he go from here?"

"That would depend on how well he knows this ship."

I turned and looked at the Captain thoughtfully. I had no idea how well Thorndike knew the ship, but there was a good chance that he knew it well. It would have been stupid of him not to learn everything there was to know about the ship before he even came aboard.

I knew that it would be foolish of me to assume that he hadn't planned for such a situation. Thorndike was smart, cunning and resourceful. He was meticulous in his planning. Getting the plans for this ship would be relatively easy. They could be gotten from almost any library, or off the Internet.

The whole thing had been well planned out. It was not likely that he would be without some plan of escape. The only thing that I could think of that he might not have foreseen was that there were three people aboard the ship who knew who he was, Tom, Monica and me. Once he found that we were aboard the ship, he did not want any of us to recognize him.

"He's on the run. He has a lot of jewelry to take with him, but none of it very big. He needs to be able to hide until he gets some place where he can get off the ship without being seen," I said more to myself than to Captain Klausen.

"I can think of two places where he could hide that would make it hard to find him. He could hide in the lowest levels of the ship where only a few of the crewmembers go, or he could hide in a cabin," I said thoughtfully.

"I only have three cabins that are not occupied," Captain Klausen said.

"Okay, we'll check those out first. However, I wasn't necessarily thinking in terms of empty cabins. He would know that those would be the first places we would check."

"You think that he might be hiding with another passenger?"

"Maybe. For one thing, we don't know if there is another person working with him or not. I kind of doubt it, but it's possible. He's a very greedy man. I believe that he has killed his partners off. But, we can't ignore the possibility that there is still another one.

"Then, there's the possibility that he is hiding out with someone who doesn't know he is a thief and a murderer. For example, the woman he went ashore with in Marquette," I added. "Thorndike can be very charming when he wants to be."

"I see your point," the Captain said as he thought about what I had suggested.

"I need to know who the woman was that he went ashore with. Do you think you could find that out for me?"

"I'm sure I can. I'll get right on it."

"In the meantime, I'm going back to my suite. Meet me there."

"Okay."

With that, the Captain left the room. As soon as he had gone, I began a complete systematic search of the room. I pulled out the drawers of the dresser and checked the bottoms of them as well as the backs to make sure nothing had been hidden on them. I stripped the bed to make sure nothing had been hidden under the covers or under the mattress. I even searched the pockets of the clothing in the closet and inside the shoes that had been left behind. I found nothing that was of interest.

I decided to take one more look at the makeup kit. I started by pulling out the drawers and emptying them out on the desk. Once I had all the drawers out, I turned the makeup kit upside down. Much to my surprise, a ring with a rather large diamond setting fell out onto the floor.

I bent down, retrieved the ring and examined it. There was no doubt in my mind that it was very old and looked to me to be very valuable. I could hardly wait to show it to Monica and have her tell me everything she could about it.

Although I knew I was closing in on Thorndike, finding the diamond ring assured me that what I had suspected was true. Oliver Higgins was Thorndike, and Thorndike was the killer of Lancaster and, most likely, Mr. Parris. It also assured me that he was ready to kill again if anyone tried to stop him.

It didn't take long to finish my search of the cabin. I found nothing more of interest and decided to go back to my suite. I was followed by the two armed crewmen.

* * * *

On my way back to our suite, I stopped by Pamela's cabin to get Monica. I took a minute to explain to Tom and Pamela what was going on at the moment. I made it a point to leave out those things that didn't seem necessary and would do nothing but increase their fears.

While I was in the cabin, I did notice that Tom and Pamela were sitting very close together. I got the feeling that all this had not hurt their relationship very much, if at all. It was good to see that Pamela was trying to give Tom some support even though the whole thing scared her half to death.

I took Monica by the arm and led her to our suite. Once we were inside with the door closed, she turned to me and asked me what was going on. After she sat down on the loveseat, I gave her a more detailed explanation of what had happened when we got to Thorndike's cabin.

"I have something that I would like you to look at," I said as I reached in my pocket and pulled out the ring.

"Where did you get it?" she asked as she began examining the ring.

"I found it in a makeup kit in Thorndike's cabin. Why?"

"I think I've seen this ring before," Monica said as she examined it.

"Where? Is it from the Samuelson Collection?"

"No. It was on a ladies hand in the dining room our first evening aboard the ship."

"You're kidding?"

"No. She was an elderly woman who looked like she was very well off. I couldn't say for sure, but I got the impression that she might be traveling alone."

"Are you sure this is the ring you saw?"

"Not a hundred percent sure, but I'm pretty sure. She was sitting at the table next to us."

"Is this ring part of the stolen jewelry?"

"No, I don't think so. I'll have to check it against the lists of stolen items to be sure, but I don't think so," Monica said.

"This is one time when I hope that ring is on the list," I said, worried that it wasn't.

The way Monica looked at me indicated she had caught my meaning. She went over to the desk and picked up the lists of stolen jewelry. I waited while she checked the ring against the lists.

"It's not on the lists," she said as she turned and looked at me.

"I was afraid of that."

"You think that Thorndike took it from the woman?" Monica asked.

"Yes. And if he did, I have some serious doubts that we will find the woman alive."

"Oh, no," Monica said with a sigh.

The fact that Thorndike had that ring was a good indication that he had been with the woman. I would have bet that the woman who owned the ring was the same woman that Thorndike went ashore with in Marquette. I could only hope that she was still alive.

Just as I was about to let Monica in on what I was thinking, there was a knock on our door. I went to the door and peeked through the peephole.

"It's Captain Klausen," I said as I reached out and turned the knob of the door.

"What did you find out?" I asked as he walked into the room.

"The woman that he went ashore with is Mrs. Elizabeth B. Townsend of Cotton Grove, Iowa. She is the widow of the late Doctor David P. Townsend."

I turned and looked at Monica. I must have had the same look on my face that she had on hers. The name Townsend meant nothing to me. I turned back around and looked at Captain Klausen.

"The name doesn't ring a bell with you, does it?" he asked.

"No, I don't think so. Should it?" I asked.

"Well, I didn't recognize it at first either. That is until I remembered what I read in the paper several weeks after Thorndike was first arrested in Wisconsin at your friend's lodge."

"What are you getting at?" I asked.

"I saw it in the local paper, that is the paper from Sturgeon Bay, Wisconsin. I picked it up while I was in Green Bay waiting for orders to this ship."

"Would you mind getting to the point, Captain?" I asked impatiently.

"Sure. I never saw it come out in any other paper that I know of, but it was reported that a Mrs. E. B. Townsend from Iowa claimed the bodies of Arthur Mortimer and his wife Elinor Mortimer," Captain Klausen said.

"Elinor Mortimer was Andrew Thorndike's sister," I said as I thought about what he had told me.

"Right."

"I never knew who claimed the bodies. You think this is the same Mrs. Townsend?" I asked.

"That would be my guess. There can't be that many E. B. Townsends from Iowa."

I had to agree with him on that. If the captain was right, there was a good chance that Mrs. Townsend was mixed up in everything that was going on in some way, and it was more than simply being escorted into town by Thorndike.

"I think we best go make a call on Mrs. Townsend," I suggested.

"I'm coming along," Monica said.

Captain Klausen looked at me, then at Monica. I knew that when she used that tone of voice, there was no changing her mind.

"You stay close to me," I said.

"Don't worry, I will," she said as she took hold of my arm.

I could see on the Captain's face that he wasn't too happy about Monica coming along with us to talk to Mrs. Townsend. I would have to admit, I wasn't very happy about it, either. But I knew Monica well enough to know that there was no stopping her when she put her mind to something.

We left the room and started down the hall. The two armed crewmen followed along behind. It was pretty late and most of the passengers had been in bed for some time. I figured that we had about four hours, maybe a little less, before the sun would be up and the passengers would be coming out of their cabins to start another day of fun in the sun before we got to Thunder Bay.

We followed Captain Klausen to suite Five-twelve. It was located about mid ship on Deck 5. It was a room with an outside view and a small balcony on the port side of the ship.

Captain Klausen stopped and pointed at the door. Monica and I went to the other side of the door while the two armed crewmen stood behind the Captain and waited for orders.

As soon as everyone was ready, I reached out and knocked on the door. I didn't get an answer right away. In fact, I had to knock again before I heard someone moving around inside the suite.

"Yes? What is it?"

The voice was that of a woman. She sounded as if we had awakened her.

"Mrs. Townsend?" I asked.

"Yes. Who is it?"

"Mrs. Townsend, my name is Nick McCord."

"What is it you want?" Mrs. Townsend asked, the tone of her voice indicating that she was not very happy about being disturbed at such a late hour.

"I would like to talk to you for a minute, please."

"Can't it wait until morning?"

"It's very important that I see you now."

"I'm going to call the Captain if you don't leave right now," she said with a hint of anger in her voice.

"I'm right here, Mrs. Townsend. This is Captain Klausen."

There was nothing but silence for a moment or two. I wasn't sure if she was trying to figure out what to do, or if she was trying to hide someone or something.

"I'm not dressed for company. Will you give me a minute?"

"Certainly, Mrs. Townsend," the Captain replied.

I found myself looking at the Captain. I'm sure he was wondering if he had done what I wanted him to do. It really didn't matter that much. As far as I knew it was the only way in or out of the suite.

A quick glance at my watch told me that we had about three hours to find Thorndike, or we might lose him. If we got to Thunder Bay and docked, he might find a way to get off the ship without being seen. Once he was off the ship, he would be very hard to find.

CHAPTER TWENTY

We had to wait for several minutes before we heard the sound of the suite door being unlocked. When the door opened there was a woman in her early to mid-sixties standing there practically shielded by the door. She was a good looking woman for her age. She was wearing a rather expensive robe. The top of her robe was open just a bit. Before she pulled it closed, I got a glimpse of the edge of her bra. It caught my attention because I couldn't think of one reason a woman would wear a bra to bed.

"What is it that you want that can't wait until morning?" she demanded to know, the tone of her voice indicating that she was upset over being disturbed.

"I can assure you, Mrs. Townsend, that it can't wait until morning," Captain Klausen said politely, but firmly.

"We are looking for Thorndike, Andrew Thorndike," I said.

"I don't know any Andrew Thorndike. And I can assure you that if I did, he would not be in my suite at this hour," she stated rather sharply.

"You might know him as Oliver Higgins," I said as I looked into her eyes for some kind of a reaction.

There was no doubt in my mind that she knew Thorndike. After all, she had arranged for the burial of Elinor Mortimer. She had to know that Elinor was Andrew Thorndike's sister.

She looked directly at me. I got the impression from the way she looked at me that she was wondering how much I knew. I had seen that same look on the faces of a lot of people that I had questioned over the years.

"Excuse me, but would you mind if we come inside to talk. We would prefer to cause you as little embarrassment as possible," Captain Klausen suggested as he took a step closer.

She immediately turned and looked at the Captain. While she was trying to decide what to do, I took a moment to look over her shoulder into her suite.

"Ah, no. I guess not," she replied nervously.

She had to have realized that she had little choice in the matter. She stepped back away from the door and allowed us to enter. I took the opportunity to look around. At first I saw nothing that was out of the ordinary, but now I was in a position to see her bed. I noticed that the covers of her bed were laid back as if she had just gotten out of it. But the sheets were not wrinkled like they should have been if she had been sleeping when we knocked on her door, or if she had even been lying in the bed. The pillowcases showed no signs that anyone had been lying on them, either. The bed was too neat to have been slept in, or sat on even for a little while.

"Do you know who Oliver Higgins is?" Captain Klausen asked.

"Yes, of course. We went into Marquette together."

"What can you tell us about him," I asked.

"Well, he's a gentleman. He went with me to several shops and then we took a tour together."

"What tour did you take?"

"We took the "Anatomy of A Murder" tour. We rented a carriage to take the tour. I wouldn't be able to walk that far. You know, it's the tour that takes you to different locations where the movie was made."

"Yes, I know. Where did you go after that?" I asked.

"We came back here to the ship."

I knew that she was lying. I could see it in her face, plus I already knew that they had not returned to the ship until it was almost time to sail. I found it interesting that she didn't question us about Higgins and Thorndike being one and the same person, but then she didn't have to because she already knew.

I also thought that if they had gone on the tour she said they did, Tom and Pamela would most likely have seen them. Neither Tom nor Pamela had mentioned that they had seen them, and I was sure they would have been keeping their eyes open. Of course, it was possible that they had gone on the tour without being seen by Tom or Pamela, but what caused them to get back to the ship just minutes before it was to sail?

"Do you mind if I look around a little?" I asked.

"I certainly do mind. What authority do you have to go nosing around my suite?" she said indignantly.

"Mr. McCord is currently working for the cruise line. He has my authority to search any cabin, suite or area of the ship that he deems to be necessary," Captain Klausen said flatly.

"Does he have a warrant?" she asked.

"He doesn't need one on this ship. As the Captain, I can give him permission. I have given him permission," Captain Klausen said with a tone of authority.

"Captain, have your men check out the closet and the bathroom. And have them be careful," I whispered.

The Captain didn't say anything. He stepped over close to the two armed crewmen and gave them instructions to search the suite for anyone who might be hiding, and to be very careful while doing it.

I watched as the two crewmen pulled their guns out of their holsters. Together they moved over to the bathroom and quickly opened the door. When there was no one there, they went to the closet and checked it out. There was no one hiding in there, either.

When they finished making sure that there was going to be no surprises from someone hiding in the suite, I started looking around the room. I noticed that the glass door to the sitting area was open slightly. I could hear Mrs. Townsend still stating her objections to my looking around her suite to the Captain.

I started for the sitting area outside, but stopped when I found something more interesting. I noticed a piece of jewelry partially hidden under a handkerchief on a table next to the bed.

I picked up the handkerchief to get a better look at the bracelet. It looked to me to be old and had a certain style that I had become somewhat familiar with since my visit to Tom's lodge and with the time I had spent with Monica.

"What are you doing?" I heard Mrs. Townsend say as she started across the room toward me.

"I'm looking at this bracelet. It's very unusual."

"It is unusual, and I would appreciate it if you would keep your hands off my personal property," she said as she reached for it.

"I'm sorry, but I'm going to have to have an expert take a look at it," I said as I stepped back out of her reach. "I think it may be stolen property."

My last comment caused her to stop suddenly and look at me. She seemed a little confused as if she didn't know what to say or what to do.

"That is not stolen. It was given to me by . . .,"

Her voice cracked slightly before she stopped. I got the feeling that she had just about let the cat out of the bag. Her slip of the tongue had made me wonder if maybe she had been hiding someone, namely Thorndike.

"Monica, take a look at this, please," I said as I handed the bracelet to her.

Suddenly, Mrs. Townsend turned and looked at Monica. I got the feeling that she wanted to say something, but thought better of it.

As Monica looked at the bracelet, I walked over to the Captain. He was watching Monica and Mrs. Townsend.

I turned my attention back to Monica as she examined the bracelet. I couldn't get it out of my mind that Mrs.

Townsend was hiding Thorndike, but where? He was certainly not in the suite.

"Nick," Monica called to me.

"Yes," I replied as I walked across the room toward her.

"This is one of the stolen items. I'm sure of it."

"That is not stolen from anywhere," Mrs. Townsend insisted.

"I'm afraid it is," Monica said. "It was stolen from a Milwaukee museum just this past week."

"I don't believe you," she said, the tone of her voice showing a little less confidence than she had shown earlier.

"You want to tell us where Andrew Thorndike is?" I asked.

"I don't know what you are talking about," she insisted.

"You are in possession of stolen property. That alone is enough to send you to jail for a few years," I explained.

"By the way, you will be arrested by the Canadian police when we dock at Thunder Bay. They do not care who you are, and the penalty for possession of stolen property is much harsher in Canada than it is in the United States," Captain Klausen added.

"But I'm a U. S. citizen. You can't hold me in Canada," she insisted.

"Yes, we can. This ship is currently in Canadian waters. U.S. citizen or not, you are under Canadian authority here," Captain Klausen clearly pointed out to her.

I looked at the Captain and wondered if the ship was really in Canadian waters. It didn't really matter. If she believed him, she might talk to us.

She looked at the Captain as if she was trying to decide if he was right. I doubted that she had any idea where we were. All she knew was that our next port of call was Thunder Bay, Ontario, Canada.

I noticed that she kept taking short, quick glances at the open door out onto the sitting area. I had to wonder if she was hoping that help would come from out there, or if

Thorndike had gone out that way. I had not had a chance to check it out, but I had to wonder if Thorndike had been in her suite when we came here. If he had that would have been his only way out.

As I walked over to the door to the sitting area, I drew the gun the Captain had given me from my belt. I slowly pushed the door open and looked out. There was no one there. There were a couple of chairs and a small table in the sitting area.

After glancing back at Mrs. Townsend and seeing that she was watching me very closely, I stepped out onto the sitting area. I walked out to the rail, leaned up against the railing and looked down the side of the ship. There was a small wake rolling out from the ship as it moved smoothly through the calm tranquil waters of Lake Superior. Then I leaned out over the edge of the ship a little more and looked down toward the water below.

Directly below the sitting area, on the deck below, I could see the edge of one of the lifeboats tied securely in its place. I looked down the side toward the stern of the ship where I could see the edge of another lifeboat. It, too, was secured in its place waiting for the day when it would be needed.

I suddenly found my eyes shifting from one lifeboat to the other. I had caught something in my eye, but wasn't sure what it was I was seeing. There was something about the lifeboats that was different.

At first I thought that it was because they were different. One was used as both a lifeboat and a power launch to shuttle people from the ship to shore and back again at ports where there were no docks where the ship could tie up. The other served as a lifeboat only.

It took me a while to see it, but there was something else different about them. Fortunately, there were lights on the deck below that allowed me to get a good view of the top of both lifeboats. I concentrated on them, looking at every little detail. It was then that I noticed that the canvas that covered the lifeboat directly below was not secured on one corner. It looked like it was loose near the back outside corner of the lifeboat.

I studied the lifeboat and the canvas covers on both boats. The other lifeboat's cover was secure and tied tightly. I looked around and began to wonder if someone could get down from here without falling overboard. The side of the ship was too smooth with nothing to hold onto for someone to climb down. And I didn't feel that there was enough of the lifeboat overhanging the side of the ship to allow for someone to simply drop down from the sitting area to the lifeboat below without a very strong possibility of going over the edge into the lake.

The more I looked at it, the more I realized that getting down would be tricky, but I convinced myself that it was possible. It was not only possible, but might prove rather easy if whoever was doing it had a rope to get down on.

I stepped back away from the edge of the ship and turned around. It was at that moment I noticed something laying back in the dark corner of the sitting area. It was a rope that had been pushed way back in the corner. I bent down and picked up the rope. It was immediately clear that the rope was long enough for someone to tie it to the railing and descend down the side of the ship to the lifeboats.

"I know where he is," I said as I stepped back into the suite and held up the rope. "He's in the lifeboat directly below this suite."

"Go find him. GO," Captain Klausen immediately ordered his men.

The two armed crewmen quickly turned and ran out of the suite. As they were leaving the room, Mrs. Townsend started running toward the sitting area. Monica quickly realized that she was going to try to warn Thorndike that they were on their way to get him.

Monica was between Mrs. Townsend and the sitting area. She ran for Mrs. Townsend and shoved her away from the door to the sitting area toward the bed. Mrs. Townsend ended up face down on the bed with Monica holding her down.

"You are under arrest, Mrs. Townsend," the Captain said as he quickly moved over to the bed. "You will be charged with receiving stolen property and harboring a criminal. There may be more charges when we finish with the investigation."

As soon as Monica got off Mrs. Townsend, I knew all was well. Now that everything was under control in her suite, I quickly left for the deck below to see if the crewmen had managed to capture Thorndike. As I came around the corner, I could see the crewmen putting handcuffs on Andrew Thorndike. He had apparently not resisted them. After all, there was no place for him to go, except overboard. To do that would certainly have meant his death. He had managed to trap himself in the lifeboat with no way to escape.

"Well, we meet again, Andy," I said as I walked up to him.

"You never would have caught me if you hadn't had Tom Walker here with you," he said angrily.

"Maybe, maybe not, Andy. But you are caught and you will be returned to jail. Only this time, the only way you will get out of jail is on a slab."

"You won't be able to prove that I killed those two on this ship."

"I think we can. The cut on your left arm left blood in Lancaster's cabin and on his clothes. All we have to do is match it up. A little thing called DNA will do the job very nicely for us. You will be charged with two counts of murder, two counts of robbery, and escape. And that's just for starters," I reminded him.

I could see the anger in his eyes. He had failed again in his quest for the treasure that his distant relative had stolen from travelers on the Great Lakes a hundred years ago. But I think the thing that angered him the most was the fact that I had spoiled his plans for a second time.

"You want to let me know where the jewelry you stole is hidden?" I asked knowing full well that he was not about to make it easy for me.

"Go to hell," he replied sharply.

"Take him away," I told the armed crewmen. "And make sure wherever you confine him that he is secured. I don't want him getting loose again."

"Yes, sir. He will be very secure. He will be in shackles."

I smiled as I stood on the deck and watched as they led Andrew Thorndike away to a small room in a lower level of the ship that was used as a jail cell. Once there, he would be put in irons. A guard would be placed on the room until we docked at Thunder Bay where he would be turned over to Canadian authorities.

I wasn't really sure what would happen to him from there, but at least he would be out of circulation for the rest of his life. Since he was responsible for two murders on a ship with a Canadian registry, he might be tried in Canada and jailed there.

The other possibility was that he would be taken back to Wisconsin under tight security where he would wait in a secure cell until he could be tried for his additional crimes. In the meantime, I was going to find Monica and start to live our lives together.

I returned to Mrs. Townsend's suite where I found her being escorted away by a couple of armed crewmen. It wouldn't be very long before she would be turned over to Canadian authorities, too.

"Did you get him?" Monica asked.

"Yes. They got him."

"Did he tell you where the jewelry was hidden?"

"No, but I'm sure that Captain Klausen and his men will find it and return it to the museums."

"Good. Can we resume our cruise now?" Monica asked as she took hold of my arm.

"I would think so. I do have a question for you, though."

"What is it?" she asked.

"With the way this trip has been going so far, are you sure you still want to get married now? I would understand if you decide to postpone it until after we get back," I said as we left suite five-twelve and started back to our suite.

I watched her as we walked down the passageway toward the stairwell. I was pretty sure that she was thinking about what I had said. When we reached the passageway to our suite, she stepped in front of me and stopped. I looked down into those beautiful cobalt blue eyes and waited for her to say something. A smile came over her face.

"The way I see it is everything that could go wrong has already happened. The rest of this trip should be a breeze. I think we should make the most of it. What do you think?"

"I agree," I said smiling down at her.

"In that case, yes. I still want to get married tomorrow at Thunder Bay by Captain Klausen as planned."

I wrapped my arms around her and pulled her tightly against me as I leaned down and kissed her. However, our moment of passion was interrupted when the Captain came around the corner.

"Excuse me, but I thought you might like to know that the jewelry that was stolen was found in Mrs. Townsend's trunks. It seems that she was to have them take it off the ship at Thunder Bay, where it was to be picked up by Thorndike," the Captain explained. "She was to leave the tour in Thunder Bay and go with him to England to live happily ever after."

"I'll bet Mrs. Townsend thought Thorndike would take her with him," I said. "She may never realize how close she came to being another one of Thorndike's victims. There's no doubt in my mind that he would have killed her once he had no further use for her."

"I'm sure you're right," Captain Klausen agreed. "You should be getting a pretty good size reward from the insurance companies for finding the stolen jewelry."

"Yeah, I guess we will," I said as I looked over at Monica and smiled.

"Oh, by the way. I had a short talk with our home office. They have told me that there will be a check for your services waiting for you at our office in Chicago when you arrive. They will also refund the entire cost of the cruise for you and your party. They asked me to wish you a very happy marriage and a long life together."

"Thank you, Captain," Monica replied. "Would you be so kind as to preside at our marriage tomorrow?"

"I would be honored," he said with a smile.

"By the way, Captain Klausen."

"Yes."

"Something I would really like to know. Were we in Canadian or United States waters when you told Mrs. Townsend that we were in Canadian waters?"

"To be perfectly honest, I'm not sure," he said with a smile.

I couldn't help but smile as Captain Klausen reached up and tipped his hat then turned around and left.

At that moment, Tom and Pamela came down the passageway.

"I hear that it is all over and that you caught Thorndike," Tom said.

"Yes, it is over. We can now enjoy the rest of the trip," I replied.

"But right now, I would like to have some time alone with my future husband," Monica said as she took me by the hand and led me to our suite.

I, of course, went willingly. The last thing outside our own little world I remember seeing was big grins on Tom and Pamela's faces. There was no doubt that tonight would be a night that Monica and I would remember for the rest of our days.

www.ingramcontent.com/pod-product-compliance
Lightning Source LLC
Chambersburg PA
CBHW061147170626
46809CB00003B/1011